C000050815

This is a work of Fiction. Al
fictional although based in historical ꞏᴜᴜᴜᵍᴜꞏ ꞏꞏ ᴊ ꞏꞏ
name appear in the story it is a coincidence.

Credits

Thanksto: Jackson from J.W. Editing and Marketing Services who edits my books and puts up with my idiosyncratic style, and to Dawn Spears the brilliant artist who created the cover artwork. My wife who is so supportive and believes in me. Last my dogs Blaez and Zeeva and cat Vaskr who watch me act out the fight scenes and must wonder what the hell has gotten into their boss.

Thank You For Reading!

I hope you enjoy reading this book as much as I enjoyed writing it. Reviews are so helpful to authors. I really appreciate all reviews, both positive and negative. If you want to leave one, you can do so on Amazon, through the website or Twitter.

About the Author

Christopher C Tubbs is a descendent of a long line of Dorset clay miners and has chased his family tree back to the 16th century in the Isle of Purbeck. He left school at sixteen to train as an Avionics Craftsman, has been a public speaker at conferences for most of his career in the Aerospace and Automotive industries and was one of the founders of a successful games company back in the 1990's. Now in his sixties, he finally got around to writing the story he had been dreaming about for years. Thanks to Inspiration from the great sea authors like Alexander Kent, Dewey Lambdin, Patrick O'Brian and Dudley Pope he was finally able to put digit to keyboard. He lives in the Netherlands with his wife, two Dutch Shepherds and a Norwegian Forest cat.

You can visit him on his website
www.thedorsetboy.com

The Dorset Boy Facebook page.

Or tweet him @ChristopherCTu3

The Dorset Boy Series Timeline

1792 – 1795.
Book 1. A Talent for Trouble, Mart joins the Navy as an Assistant Steward and ends up a midshipman.

1795 – 1798.
Book 2. The Special Operations Flotilla, Marty is a founder member of the Special Operations Flotilla, learns to be a spy and passes as lieutenant.

1799 – 1802.
Book 3. Agent Provocateur, Marty teams up with Linette to infiltrate Paris, marries Caroline, becomes a father and fights pirates in Madagascar.

1802 – 1804.
Book 4. In Dangerous Company, Marty and Caroline are in India helping out Arthur Wellesley, combating French efforts to disrupt the East India Company and French sponsored pirates on Reunion. James Stockley born

1804 – 1805.
Book 5. The Tempest, piracy in the Caribbean, French interference, Spanish gold and the death of Nelson. Marty makes Captain.

1806 – 1807.
Book 6. Vendetta, A favour carried out for a prince, a new ship, the S.O.F. move to Gibraltar, the battle of Maida, counter espionage in Malta and a Vendetta declared and closed.

Contents

Chapter 1: Madras

Marty and Caroline walked through the market in Madras enjoying the exotic and somewhat alien sights and sounds. The air was rich with the scent of exotic spices; cumin, coriander, aniseed, pepper and more, all of which would cost a king's ransom back in England. Caroline was looking at using Marty's status as a shareholder in the East India Company to import spices to England. She would distribute them through the same network she used for the wine and brandy she distributed for the Deal boys.

Marty carried their daughter Bethany in his arms as proud a young father as could be, pointing things out to her as they passed each stall in turn. Beth in turn gurgled, giggled and sometimes gawped as things caught her eye.

An experienced observer would note that the couple were escorted, at a discrete distance behind them, by two dangerous looking men. A really expert one would also spot two that walked thirty feet in front of them.

Caroline stopped at a silk merchants stall and looked at a delicate blue bolt of silk.

"That would be just perfect for a gown for the Governor's ball next week." she exclaimed.

"*What does this cost?*" Marty asked the merchant in Hindi. He had been studying the local language and achieved a working proficiency in it.

"*Oh, Sahib this is the very best silk, perfect for making saris and only one anglina a yard,*" the merchant boasted. An anglina was a silver coin and was worth around a shilling.

"*Don't think I am a fool and you can rob me,*" Marty replied. "*I think it is worth no more than twenty cupperoon a yard.*" A cupperoon was a copper coin and fifty cupperoon made an anglina.

"Oh, Sahib is very wise, is blessed with a beautiful wife and a beauteous baby and surely knows that this wonderful silk is worth at least forty cupperoon a yard."

Marty was enjoying himself but a sharp nudge from Caroline's elbow brought him up short.

"I will pay thirty and no more," he offered splitting the difference, knowing he could have gone lower. The merchant agreed and Caroline asked for ten yards. Marty beckoned to a young Indian boy who was standing nearby watching them hopefully.

"Do you want to earn a cupperoon?"

The boy nodded vigorously, and Marty handed him the roll of silk.

They bought a number of other items and ended up with a small group of children following them carrying packages. They were led by the strutting boy who was first and had made himself the leader of their baggage train.

Back at their bungalow Caroline sent for her dressmaker. A talented Indian lady who was able to make western style clothes from silk, which was a notoriously difficult fabric to work with. They ensconced themselves in her bedroom to create the ball gown that Caroline had imagined.

Marty in the meantime was in his study entertaining an Officer of the Company Marine.

Edward Cooper Esq. was the thirty-year-old Captain of the company frigate Endeavour.

"When do we leave for Réunion?" he asked, eager to complete their mission to root out and destroy the pirates that used the French held island in the Indian Ocean.

"Not until after that damned ball," Marty replied, "we should have the intelligence from the Belle by then."

The Belle was a brig that had been captured the year before. It had made the mistake of attacking the East Indiaman that had carried Marty and Caroline to India. Since then she had been repaired and bought into the Marine.

Marty had been asked to come up with a plan to pacify the pirates working out of Réunion and had tasked the brig to reconnoitre the island. He hoped the Marine captain had the guile to use the fact that the brig was a former pirate ship to get in close.

Meanwhile he had to be Lord Candor, not Lieutenant Stockley Royal Navy, and attend the Governor's ball.

As soon as Cooper left, Caroline had a servant fetch Marty for a fitting of a new suit she was having made for him. He stood impatiently as the little Indian tailor fussed over the fit of the suit which was cunningly made of lightweight material but looked like the current fashion in London. It had taken Caroline quite a while and a lot of patience to get the tailor to understand what she wanted, but they had got there in the end.

There was a childish shriek from the door and one-year old Beth toddled in pursued by her nurse. Since she had learned to walk, she was a terror for exploring and would make her escape whenever they took their eyes off her. Mary, her nurse, was in hot pursuit and scooped her up before she managed to get into the tailor's box of scissors and pins.

"Is this really necessary?" Marty grumbled for the umpteenth time. "I thought the last fitting would do it."

"Be patient my love, you must look your absolute best. They will be looking at us and wondering how two commoners managed to end up as Baron and Baroness Candor. We will not give them an inch to work with."

The fact was, that they didn't have an ounce of noble blood between them. Caroline had the title through an arranged marriage to the elderly, and now late, Lord Candor who had died just two years after marrying her when she was just sixteen years old. She had scandalised society with a string of lovers after that until Marty fought a duel for her. They had become lovers and when she fell pregnant with Beth they had married.

The big surprise was that the British Monarch, King George the third, had not only blessed the marriage but confirmed Marty in the Barony and made him a Knight of the Bath as well. They were admired by some but condemned by many others as new blood. Marty's reputation as a dualist kept the comments to the background but Caroline was sensitive to them.

Marty had been tasked by Admiral Lord Hood and William Wickham to go to India and help the East India Company counter the threat posed by French sponsored rebellions and piracy. Caroline had insisted on going with him as it was likely to be at least a three-year posting. So now he was stood there like some kind of tailor's dummy.

The night of the ball came around and once he was dressed, he had to admit that the suit did do justice to his physique. It showed off his shoulders and it was cunningly cut to hide the fact he was carrying his fighting knife in a shoulder sheath under his left arm. Marty never went anywhere unarmed. He wore a sash with his order of the garter on it and the diamond broach with his coat of arms the Prince Regent had given him as a wedding present.

Caroline was dressed in the light blue silk ballgown that showed off her figure. The colour set off her auburn hair and her diamond earrings, tiara and necklace complemented the broach the Prince had given her. She carried a small handbag which had a muff pistol hidden inside it.

Their carriage stopped outside the governor's mansion which was brightly lit with torches and lanterns and was met by small army of servants buzzing around the entrance helping the guests. The sound of an orchestra wafted through the air along with the scent of flowers on the night breeze. Cicadas provided a background hum that Marty found quite pleasant.

They were announced and the room hushed as people turned to look. Caroline stepped forward, giving Marty no choice but to step with her, and smiled dazzlingly at the assembled crowd. The chatter restarted. They greeted several people before they came up to Governor Armstrong and his wife.

"Lady Caroline!" his wife greeted her, "you look absolutely ravishing. You will cost all the husbands a fortune and make your seamstress wealthy when all the ladies copy you."

"She is an absolute wizard with silk." Caroline smiled keen to make sure her lady did well. "I will let you have her address."

"Milord Candor. Good to see you." Armstrong said in a rich baritone. He was a large man who had probably been quite muscular in his youth but was tending to portliness as he aged. "You two have caused quite a stir amongst the British community."

"We have?" replied Marty looking slightly confused.

"Well, yes." Armstrong clarified. "Your wedding was heavily featured in the newspapers and the ladies were all a swoon at the romance. Now you are here in the flesh and they can see that you are as handsome a couple as the press reported."

"Any news of the Belle?" Marty asked to change the subject.

Armstrong took the hint and said that she was expected any day now.

Ranjit Sihng, a senior advisor to the Company and a fellow passenger on the voyage from England, wandered over with his wife and greeted Marty and Caroline. He had become their friend during the trip and he and Marty were regular sparing partners at weapons practice.

"Caroline, you shine like a beautiful star," smiled Surinda, "and Marty that suit is fantastic, who is your tailor? I want to have one made for Ranjit."

Ranjit didn't look too keen on that idea.

The Governor rescued him by suggesting that they leave the ladies and take a few minutes to talk about the upcoming campaign. They left them and went to the Governor's study where they were joined by Captain Cooper.

"What is the plan once the Belle returns?" asked Armstrong.

"Well, depending on what they report, we will take at least her and the Endeavour back to Réunion. I would like a cutter as well if she could be armed with carronades."

"Why do you need a cutter? Isn't that a bit small for this work?" asked Captain Cooper.

Ranjit laughed. "Martin beat three French luggers with a cutter and they cleaned out the Madagascar pirates with a cutter and a sloop."

How did he know that? Marty thought.

"Really?" Cooper exclaimed. "You must tell me that story."

"Later, when we have time." Marty replied. "A cutter can get in and out of places a brig or a frigate can't. It's nimble so it can harass the enemy and if it's got carronades it can deliver a punch much greater than its size."

"I will ask the Commodore," the Governor replied convinced by Marty's assuredness.

"Lord Candor will be responsible for strategy and training and will have overall command of the squadron," Captain Copper stated. Marty saw in his eyes, and the way he looked at him, that he was a little put out to be under the command of such a young man. Even if he was a Lord.

"He may be young, but he has more combat experience than men twice his age according to Lord Hood," replied the

Governor, "and the Company commissioners have great faith in him."

"And I have seen him fight," added Ranjit. "Don't worry you are in good hands."

"Will you be accompanying us Ranjit?" Marty asked.

"Yes, the Company has asked me to act as an observer." He replied with a grin.

After discussing a few more mundane issues they re-joined the ladies. Caroline was looking cross and Armstrong's wife was livid.

"What's got you all in a knot?" Marty asked

"That stuck up, good for nothing, blue blooded arse of a captain of the fifth regiment just called me a pretend Baroness and said I shouldn't be seen in public" Caroline seethed.

"That would be Captain Fortesque-Parker," Governor Armstrong observed. "He is distantly related to the Duke of Marlborough on his mother's side, has a very elevated idea of his own nobility and a low tolerance for alcohol," he added with a sneer.

'Damn, why can't they just accept us for what we are?' Marty thought.

"Well I can't let that go," he said slightly regretfully, "with your permission sir?" Armstrong nodded.

He walked up to the offender and tapped him on the shoulder. He was a bit taller than Marty with thin brown hair, long nose, weak chin and slightly protruding teeth. As soon as they made eye contact, Marty punched him squarely on the jaw to gasps from the surrounding ladies.

Fortesque-Parker landed on his rump with the contents of his wine glass spilled over his shirt.

"No one insults my wife," Marty said in a cold voice, "if they do, they insult me as well. I will meet you on the field of honour at your earliest convenience. My seconds will call on you in the morning, unless you wish to settle this here and now?"

Fortesque-Parker looked at Marty in astonishment and then fear as he saw the steel in his eye. He looked over at Caroline who was grinning openly.

"Well?" asked Marty impatiently.

"Oh! Well yes!" he stammered.

"Yes now? Or Yes in the morning?"

"Oh! The morning. Of course, seconds in the morning!" he finally got out.

Marty turned and stalked back to Caroline. She was grinning wolfishly at him.

"I think he nearly wet himself. Do you think he will go through with it?" she asked.

"His regiment will not let him do other than go through with the duel," the Governor stated. "They value regimental honour above all else!"

"Can I act as one of your seconds?" Ragit asked.

"Thank you, yes." Marty replied.

"I will be the other." Cooper insisted.

"Thank you as well." Marty shook both their hands and they left to talk to Fortesque-Parker to find out when and where they should meet his seconds.

The next afternoon Rangit and Cooper, his seconds, arrived at their bungalow.

"He wants it to be pistols." Ranjit told him. "We set the time for tomorrow morning at dawn on the beach to the north of the town."

"Aye we also limited it to one shot each at twenty paces separation." Cooper added. "I checked and he is supposed to be a fair shot with a rifle. Likes to hunt. No information on his ability with a pistol."

Marty grinned. "Animals don't shoot back."

"You are very cheerful for someone who is going to be shot at," Ranjit observed wryly.

"It is all about the edge my friend." Marty replied. "Mine is he has heard about my, so called, reputation. That will be in his mind all night."

The next morning, they left before dawn. Caroline came with them, leaving Beth at home. Blaez was left behind, sleeping in the nursery in his usual place under her cot.

Clive Fortesque-Parker and his seconds arrived at the beach in plenty of time. When Lord Candor and his party arrived, the huge Sikh had the pistols. A fine pair of Manton's with walnut stocks, browned barrels and silver inlaid actions. They were fifteen inches long and had rudimentary rear-sights. They were perfectly balanced.

One of his seconds went with the Sikh and prepared the guns, taking care to ensure the load was identical in each. As usual there was a surgeon and master of ceremonies in attendance.

Clive was regretting ever opening his mouth. He blamed the drink, but it was a combination of that and his resentment at being a non-titled member of the Marlborough clan that had pushed him into it. Once said he couldn't retract it without losing face, and his fellow officers wouldn't allow that slur on their regiment. It was so unfair that those two peasants had titles and he didn't.

The combatants were called forward and Lord Candor chose his weapon first. He grinned at Clive as if he hadn't a care in the world, which unnerved him. *Does the man have no fear?* he thought, sweating.

They walked side by side to the designated area, Lord Candor humming a jolly tune. Then they were positioned back to back on the beach. Clive had chosen to walk North.

The Master of Ceremonies counted the steps off. At the count of ten Clive turned with his pistol held barrel up. He stared down range at his opponent and saw that he was looking him directly in the eyes. He didn't blink or move to aim his pistol as Clive brought his gun to bear.

He could feel the sweat on his brow and the tremble of his hand as he tried to aim it. All Lord Candor did was raise his empty left hand at him like he held a gun and mimed shooting. Clive couldn't believe he was letting him have first shot.

"Bang" Candor said loud enough to be heard. Clive jumped, blinking rapidly, and his pistol fired unexpectedly as his finger tightened on the hair trigger. The bullet missed Lord Candor by a good foot.

Clive was now stood facing a man known to be a killer, with a loaded pistol in his hand, and was no longer grinning at him. Who slowly brought his gun into firing position, his hand steady as a rock, he did not blink.

Clive had never faced an armed enemy. His father had bought him his rank and he had only commanded parade soldiers up to then.

How did I come to this he thought in despair!

Candor had completed the transition from pistol at rest to it pointing straight at his face.

Time seemed to slow to a crawl.

His vision zoomed in on the gaping maw of the pistol.

He could see straight down the barrel!

He watched in horror as the trigger finger slowly tightened.

The hammer dropped and the flint sparked on the frizzen. The priming powder ignited.

He fainted.

The bullet passed over his head as Marty pulled the barrel up at the last moment.

He came too as someone put smelling salts under his nose. It was one of his seconds. There was no sign of Marty or his people.

He knew he would be leaving India on the next available ship.

Back at the villa Marty and his entourage were in good spirits.

"Bang?" Wilson asked as he was told the story of the morning.

"Yes, he made a mime of shooting him with his empty left hand and said 'bang'." Captain Cooper said. "Never seen anything like it."

"Then he fainted?" Wilson asked again.

"Yes, out like a light."

Wilson laughed. "Typical of Martin. Dominate his opponent, get an edge and exploit it to the full."

Cooper was rapidly re-assessing the young man he would be following into battle with the pirates based out of Réunion.

Chapter 2: Intelligence

The Belle returned with Tom and John Smith bringing Marty's team back up to its full strength of eight. It had grown by two when the two Basques, who had joined them during the mission to disrupt French efforts to ferment rebellion, had insisted on staying with him. More importantly they had a comprehensive report on the harbour at Réunion.

"It's a precious long way to Réunion from here, over two and an 'alf thousand sea miles we logged. The port is on the Northern end of the island and is called La Possession. It's flying the French flag an there be two French frigates there, one thirty-eight and t'other a forty," Tom reported to the gathering that included, Marty, The Governor, Ranjit, General Lake, Captain Cooper, Captain Purvis of the Belle and Lieutenant Jarrow of the Cutter Jolly.

"There were also two brigantines, a xebec and what looked like a corvette all under different colours," John Smith added.

"That is a lot of ships for us to take on," observed Captain Cooper.

"All at once, yes." Marty replied. "Carry on Tom."

"Aye sir. The frigates looked settled, with yards crossed and harbour gaskets fitted. Not tidy like a British ship mind. The others were ready for sea."

"It would be good if we could remove those frigates before Napoleon sues for peace," General Lake put in.

"Easier said than done," Cooper snorted. "They are both bigger than the Endeavour which is a thirty-six."

Marty sat back and grinned at the assembled men.

"It's not the size of the dog, it's how hard it bites. Our rate of fire will more than make up for our lack of guns," he reassured them. "Now I need to talk to our French guest."

The 'French guest' was a French agent that they had captured whilst foiling an attempted arms shipment to fuel a rebellion. Nobody from the French government had made

17

any comment about his incarceration, or the operation in general, so they suspected that the whole thing had been run under a cloak of 'plausible deniability.'

"In other words, you have been hung out to dry my friend." Marty said to Brieu. *"That means you are mine to do with as I want."*

Brieu said nothing just looked at the table top.

"Do you know Federick La Plant? He was at the Rotterdam consulate."

There was just a flicker in Brieu's eyes.

"I killed him for torturing my friend, who I had to kill to put out of his pain. Then I tortured Arnoud St Pierre until he gave up all his secrets."

He took out his fighting knife and examined the edge.

"I will peel your skin from your body inch by inch with a cat o' nine tails and rub salt into what is left until you tell me everything you know."

He looked him square in the eyes. Then he smiled. Brieu thought it was the most chilling thing he had ever seen.

"Now I want to know everything about the operation in Mahé and everything you know about Réunion."

Brieu looked down at the table top again.

Marty sighed and called out.

"Bring in the grating and salt!"

The door opened and Christo and Matai entered carrying a ship's grating. Antton followed with a bucket of salt.

"My men are Basques you know. They have no love for the French who want to destroy their homeland."

"Strip him and lash him to the grating" he ordered.

Brieu put up a fight but Garai joined them and together they got the struggling man secured.

Marty took of his jacket and rolled up the sleeves of his shirt. He picked up his knife and tested the edge. Then took out a wet stone and honed it a little more, the noise grating on

Brieu's nerves. When he could shave the hairs off his arm he nodded in satisfaction.

"I don't want you to say anything right now as I'm going to give you a taste of what is to come if you stay silent," he whispered in Brieu's ear.

He nodded to Garai who took a cat out of its baize bag and shook out the knotted thongs so that Brieu could get a good look at them. He then rubbed salt into the thongs from the bucket.

"You have never seen a cat before?" Marty asked. *"It will strip the skin from your back and cut your flesh to the bone."*

He held up his hand with two fingers extended. Garai pulled back his arm and brought the cat down on Brieu's back.

Unlike all British sailors, who knew exactly what a cat could do and the pain it could inflict from either personal experience of from witnessing a punishment, Brieu had no idea of what to expect. As the cat struck his eyes popped open and he screamed.

Garai delivered a second lash and this time put his shoulder behind it. Brieu screamed again.

Marty pulled his head around by his hair and asked softly.

"Tell me about Mahé."

Tears were running down Brieu's face. The salt that Garai had rubbed into the lashes was burning his back.

"Will you tell me what I want to know?"

He shook his head.

"It only gets worse. After ten lashes we will give the cat to a left-handed man. You know him. The big man who came with the soldiers. That will leave a lovely checkerboard pattern on your back."

He nodded to Garai.

Eight more times the lash fell and then Marty picked up a handful of salt and gently rubbed it into the cuts on his back.

Brieu arched his back in agony.

Marty called for Wilson.

The thought of Wilson wielding the lash was enough and Brieu said.

"Stop! *I will tell you everything!"*

"Good man," Marty praised him. *"I knew you would see it my way."*

"There are three agents who are responsible for fermenting the rebellion," Marty reported to the Governor, Ranjit Sihng and Captain Cooper.

"Brieu was one. Each was given a leader to deal with. Brieu had Oomaithurai. The other two have Marutha Pandiyar and Kerala Simham. The plan was for Oomaithurai to raise an army, armed with the guns we intercepted and reinforced by men from the other two groups. The agents regularly return to Mahé to file reports so you may be able to intercept them en-route. The details are in our report."

"Your methods are very, aah, direct, Martin," General Lake said with a disapproving look.

"Not as direct as theirs," he responded. "They tortured a friend of mine near to death. In comparison we were gentle."

The General nodded but was obviously uncomfortable with the idea. He completely missed the irony that his sergeants regularly beat his troops for ill-discipline and ten strokes was considered mild.

Captain Cooper changed the subject.

"What did you learn about Réunion?" he asked

"It's set up to disrupt the East India Company. The two Frigates are there to protect the island in case we decide to attack it. The other ships are supposed to be French privateers with letters of marque.

The Tanya, as the Belle was named when she was captured, was the only non-French ship there. According to the crew we captured, the ones who got a pardon for helping with the infiltration of Mahé, Jerimiah Flann was the pirate king until the French showed up. He wasn't allowed to join the club and Billy Smith reckoned that all the other ships weren't privateers at all but country ships posing as them."

"Wouldn't Brieu know that?" asked the Governor.

"Not necessarily," Marty replied thoughtfully. "French departments don't really talk to each other that much. He said he got instructions to help them as required, but each of them is playing their own game. Billy thought the way the ships were run was more Navy like than privateer. The number of crew is lower than you would expect as well."

"I don't understand that. Can you explain?" asked Ranjit.

"Privateers carry up to double crew the normal crew so they can man as many prizes as possible. They also prefer to get in close and board, relying on superior numbers to carry the day."

"Does this make a difference to your thoughts on how to defeat them?" asked Armstrong.

"Not really. I have no intention of boarding them unless we have to. I would rather rely on our superior gunnery and sail handling," Marty responded.

"What we need to do is lure them out and take them one or two at a time then" Cooper stated.

Chapter 3: To Spring a Trap

Marty visited the Company's shipping office the next day and got the schedule of departures for the next two months. He was surprised it was so easily obtainable. Security was not something that came to the minds of the Company clerks before the prospect of making a profit.

There were a couple of ships that were leaving at the right time for them to be used as bait. He went to talk to the captains.

"Let me get this straight." Captain Smedley of the Amethyst summarised. "You want me to make it known I will take the eastern passage between Madagascar and Reunion, but I don't actually have to. Just go in that direction long enough to be seen to be doing it."

"Yes, that just about sums it up," Marty replied with a smile.

"This is just to tempt the pirates in Réunion out so you can give them a hiding. But won't they just turn tail as soon as they see you with your warships?"

"That is a risk," Marty replied truthfully.

"Well it would be better if I took that passage and we arrange to give them a nasty surprise when they take me on" Smedley continued

"That is true, but I can't ask a Company captain to risk his ship and cargo" Marty admitted.

"Well that is surely my risk to take, but I will ask how you plan to give them a bloody nose."

"Well if you are offering, what I propose is that we beef up your crew with me and my men plus a few company marines. We upgrade your guns with some carronades on your fore and quarterdeck. We let the French get in close and engage them, holding them up until the Marine ships can come to our assistance. They will be positioned hull down on the horizon ready to close in as soon as they hear gunfire. If they are positioned correctly, they will be just able to see us from their mast tops," Marty extemporised.

"We will need to keep them engaged for about two hours," Smedley estimated.

"Yes, probably less but no longer than that," Marty replied.

"I'd be happier if we had one ship in closer support," Smedley stated.

Marty considered that.

"We could make the Belle look like a cargo ship. That would even things up against most of what they have got. You have twenty-four guns?"

"Yes, six pounders."

"Humph, they are next to useless. We will upgrade you to nines plus thirty-two-pound carronades. Can you make an excuse to get your ship into dock for some kind of repair?"

A week later and Marty was stood on the deck of the Amethyst in the Company repair dock. A team made a show of replacing the main mast stays which Captain Smedley had condemned as unsafe. Under cover of darkness the ship's armament had been removed and would be replaced that night with long nines and carronades.

A supplementary crew of Company gunners and marines were already onboard effectively doubling the manpower. All the scheduled passengers had been re-booked on other ships and their cabins were now utilised to accommodate the extra crew.

The Belle had been given a makeover and now looked just like a merchant brig. The paintwork had been done in such a way as to disguise the gun ports rather than enhance them. She had also been given an armament upgrade and now sported:

Eight long nines, four to a side amidships.

Ten twenty-four-pound carronades, five to a side filling the fore and aft ports.

Four thirty-two-pound carronades, two on the fore deck and two on the quarterdeck.

The two ships together would give a pirate a very nasty surprise if he was in anything smaller than a frigate and even then, could probably hold their own.

The rest of their 'squadron' was waiting in the harbour. The frigate Endeavour, and the cutter Jolly were fully provisioned and ready to go.

The time came for them to set sail. The Amethyst and the Belle left first and dawdled south as merchant ships did. The Endeavour and the Jolly left three hours later. Captain Cooper brought the Endeavour up behind the two lead ships so his main mast lookout could just see them. With the height his mast gave them that put them around twelve miles behind and with all sail set they could catch up in less than an hour. It also reduced the chance that anyone would be able to spot them, but it would take careful sailing to stay out of sight.

Captain Smedley steered a course Southeast that would take them between Madagascar and the island of Réunion. They expected to attract attention when they got level with the northern tip of Madagascar.

Smedley surprised Marty by keeping sail on overnight thereby averaging around ten knots. When he asked him, he said he only reduced sail when he had passengers onboard, for their comfort. They made a good two hundred fifty to three hundred miles a day.

Ten days of reasonable weather saw them in their hunting grounds, and they doubled the watch, changing them every hour. Marty was sure the 'pirates' had people watching the harbour and fast ships to carry messages so expected company at some time.

They were one hundred miles West-Northwest of Réunion when the hail came.

"Sail off the larboard bow!"

The maintained their course and thirty minutes later came,

"Sail on the larboard bow has turned towards us. Second sail dead ahead."

"They had two ships positioned horizon to horizon looking for us," Marty observed.

"Looks like it," replied Smedley.

"I'm going up for a look," Marty informed him.

He slung a bring-em-near over his shoulder and ran up the mainmast ratlines, around the futtock shrouds to the topsail yard where the lookout was perched. He settled in and scanned the horizon with just his naked eye. He spotted the sail off the larboard bow easily and then after a moment of scanning saw the one dead ahead. Then he brought up the bring-em-near to his eye and scanned again.

Now he could see that the first ship was a corvette. He scanned right and picked up the second. It was a xebec. To be sure he scanned further right and stopped. There was a third sail off the bow to starboard. Probably a brigantine from the fact she had a gaff sail on her main. All three were converging on them.

Marty arrived on the quarterdeck via a stay and went to talk with Smedley.

"Three of them, you say!" Smedley exclaimed.

"Yes, they had them strung out to cover as much sea area as possible but now they are converging on us. I think they will try and get here at the same time hoping to overwhelm us with numbers and avoid a fight if possible."

"We will have to disappoint them then." Smedley said with a grin.

"Just continue as if we haven't seen them for another hour and then do what any good merchantman would do." Marty replied.

"Turn and make a run for it," Smedley laughed, "but not too fast."

"Smart one that for a cart driver," Tom observed to Marty as they stood together looking over the guns, "and he's game."

"He is at that," Marty laughed. "A frustrated frigate captain."

"Does the Belle know what to do?" Tom asked.

"Yes, they will make as if they are running away, then as soon as the French engage the Amethyst, they will run in and try and get one or those buggers between them and us," Marty explained.

"And we will deal them a double dose of iron," Tom smiled happily.

"We have to try and keep them all occupied until the Endeavour and Jolly arrive."

The time came for them to turn and run. They made a lubberly wear rather than tacking. Making a show of poor sail handling.

The three ships closed in rapidly and Smedley steered Northeast to bring them closer to their support. As they were about to be caught the Belle veered off making as much sail as she could and looked to be abandoning its larger consort.

The xebec and the brigantine stayed on the Amethyst while the corvette chased after the Belle.

Neither the xebec or the brigantine had bow chasers, so they tried to get up alongside to bring their broadsides to bear. The Amethyst's sail handling suddenly improved and she maintained her lead over the xebec. The brigantine, being the nimbler of the two, started to pull up alongside.

The Belle did what only a brig could do and reversed course in almost her own length catching the corvette by surprise. Their captain tried to do the same but just managed to put them in irons.

The Belle raced down and swung around to sandwich the brigantine between them.

"RUN OUT!" Marty called and the men hauled up the ports and ran out the preloaded guns. They had double shotted the nines with reduced charge to prevent the shot passing through their target. The carronades were loaded with the big smasher balls."

"As you bear. FIRE!"

The gun captains had been instructed to aim at the hull twixt wind and water. Both ships fired at the same time.

The brigantine didn't stand a chance. The combined broadsides of both the Endeavour and the Belle ripped through her thin hull like tissue paper. The smasher balls causing utter devastation, a number hit at the waterline. She shuddered and slowed. Crippled by the weight of water pouring into her hull.

The xebec had pulled up alongside and hadn't seen what had happened. She fired a broadside aimed at taking down the Amethyst's rigging.

She partly succeeded. The main mast rigging was damaged, and the top mast fell to the deck. The lookout fell, screaming, landing across the rail and bouncing over the side.

Marty had the crews switch sides and ran out the starboard battery. They fired and the xebec shuddered as a number of hits made their mark. However, he had the wind gauge and opened the distance to cancel out the advantage of their smashers. That confirmed to Martin that this was no ordinary pirate.

He looked over to the Belle and saw she was hotly engaged with the corvette, then looked to the North to see where their support was. He could see the Endeavour, hull up and closing. She was carrying every stitch of sail she could carry, and Marty guessed that he needed to keep contact with the xebec for at least another thirty minutes.

He went to talk to Captain Smedley who was on the quarterdeck and looked to be enjoying himself immensely.

"Exiting stuff!" he called to Marty as he mounted the steps to the quarterdeck. His face was flushed and his eyes bright.

"Certainly is!" laughed Marty. He indicated the approaching Endeavour. "Keep us between the xebec and them if you can. We need them to be closer before the xebec runs for it."

"You think he will?" Smedley asked.

"Once he sees them, he will. He won't want to take on a frigate, but if we can hold him up long enough and damage his rigging then they will stand a good chance of catching him."

Smedley looked up at his damaged top mast and frowned.

"I owe him for that and the loss of my man."

"We may lose a few more before we are done," Marty sighed.

They kept up a slugging match for about ten minutes when, quite unobserved, the cutter Jolly suddenly appeared and raked the corvette's stern. That ended that fight and all of a sudden it was three to one against the xebec. She ran.

The Endeavour was only a mile away by then having made better than thirteen knots in her efforts to get into the fight. She gave chase and it was clear she would catch her prey fairly quickly.

They had a captain's meeting on the Endeavour. The xebec and corvette were laying to amidst the squadron.

"We still have two frigates and a brigantine to deal with," Marty opened. "and the Amethyst needs to continue her voyage."

"Damned if I do!" spluttered Captain Smedley. "I've seen this through this far and I will see the damn thing through to the end!"

Captain Cooper clapped him on the shoulder and said,

"Damned if you're not more than welcome!" causing a laugh from the others.

"Well I've only got dry goods in my hold. Spices, tea and silk."

Marty coughed as he realised it was probably Caroline's spices that were at risk. *'She will not be amused if I get them sunk,'* he thought.

"It's all insured." Smedley added.

'Oh, that's alright then,' Marty thought, only a little sarcastically.

"We still have the same problem," Cooper stated emphatically. "We can't take on both frigates and the brigantine at the same time!"

"What if we don't have to?" Marty asked.

"Don't have to what?" Cooper asked back.

"Don't have to fight them." Marty replied. "They are safe and secure in their harbour. Tom, what were the defences again?"

"There is a harbour on the West side which is mainly used for fishing and is largely undefended. The main harbour is here on the North side," he pointed to the location on the map that they had made from their recce. "That one is defended by a redoubt along either side of this entrance. There be six, twenty-four-pound pieces on the west side and four on the east. They also have ovens for heating shot"

"That would make a direct attack suicidal," Stanley, the captain of the Belle observed.

"They be set up fer defending an attack from the sea." Tom started to say.

"But not from the land!" Marty and Cooper finished with him.

"What we need is a distraction to keep them looking out to sea." Marty observed.

Chapter 4: Fiery Retribution.

The captured xebec and corvette smelled of oil and their lower decks were piled with anything flammable that Marty and his men could find. All the guns were triple shotted and double charged. A volunteer crew of just five men on each sailed them towards the main harbour mouth. It was two hours before dawn.

Three hours earlier the boats from all the ships in the squadron, less two boats which were towed behind the xebec and the corvette for the crews to escape, had been loaded with heavily armed men. They had been towed to within two miles of the fishing harbour and then cut loose to row in. There was a moderate swell and scudding clouds. The moon was new and it, with the stars, provided just enough light to be able to see the outline of the island.

Oarlocks were padded with rags to avoid noise and they slowed the stroke rate as they got closer inshore to reduce any splash. They had arrived slightly South of the entrance and had to row against the prevailing current to get up into position. They were just twenty minutes later than planned.

Two boats took the lead and slipped into the harbour ahead of the rest. In one was Marty and his team with Ranjit and in the other a squad of marines led by their lieutenant. Their faces were blackened with burnt cork and they were all dressed in dark clothes.

That had actually been the hardest part of the planning. The marine lieutenant had been very reluctant to give up their uniforms. He considered it dishonourable to go to war in anything other than full uniform. In exasperation Marty had threatened to have him and his men left out of the whole exercise and replaced with 'lesser' men who had more sense. Evidently the thought of being left out of the fight was worse than being out of uniform and he had given in.

As they approached the entrance, they spotted a sentry walking along the wall. Marty stood, took a shepherd's sling from his belt and fitted a musket ball in the cup. He swung it around above his head and then launched the ball with a flick of his wrist. He had been practicing with the sling for a couple of years now and the bullet flew straight and true taking the sentry in the side of the head. He dropped to the floor without a sound.

Marty's boat went right and the marine's left. They pulled up to the harbour walls either side of the entrance, swiftly scaled them and swarmed along the top clearing anyone they found out of the way.

By the time the other boats came through the entrance the advance team had secured the harbour, and they were able to disembark at the jetty. The men spread out with the marines and Marty's team in the lead.

Two of the marines who had been woodsmen (poachers) in the past ranged ahead dealing with any unfortunates who were up and about at that hour.

Marty checked his watch; they were still running a bit later than planned but it was within limits.

They made their way through the fishermen's huts and into the main town. It was only a mile and a half, and they tried to make as little sound as possible. If anybody did spot them, they didn't raise the alarm.

Every now and then they came upon a dead native or sailor that the advance team had made sure of.

When they reached the harbour, they formed into three groups. One went to the entrance of the redoubt to the west of the harbour, one to the east and the other made their way down to the dock. They concealed themselves and waited until they saw a flickering pair of lights approaching from the sea. The xebec and the corvette were approaching. The crew had set them on fire half a mile out turning them into fire ships which were now heading straight for the harbour entrance.

A bell rung furiously on one of the frigates as the alarm was sounded. Lights started to burn in the town and the gunners left their barracks running towards the redoubts. Marty let them; it would be easier to take them one gun at a time than en mass.

Each of the guns was separated from the next by an earth wall to protect the crews against any accidental explosions. *'Bloody silly idea* thought Marty *but useful for us.'* Marty's sling whirled and a man dropped, he signalled and his men rushed forward.

As it turned out the gunners weren't well armed and soon succumbed to the determined attack by the British. Once they had control, Marty had the men manhandle two of the big guns around to point into the harbour.

The French seemed to have the shot ovens permanently fired as far as they could tell and had shot loaded in them already glowing red hot. He wouldn't look a gift horse in the mouth, and soon had his men loading the guns with the red-hot shot.

Up to that point the frigate crews had been transfixed by the sight of two of their own ships coming into the harbour ablaze, but with shouted commands the officers got the ships swung around on their springs to bring their guns to bear. Some of the guns ran out and they let off a ragged, partial broadside. Half their crews were ashore on leave!

As they fired Marty, and the crew that had taken the other redoubt, fired their guns. The red-hot shot smashed into the nearest frigate and at point blank range ripped through the hull and out the other side.

"Half the charge!" Marty yelled. He wanted the balls to stay in the hull and start a fire, not go through.

The impact of the shot got the attention of the frigates. They now faced a dilemma, turn their guns on the shore battery or try and stop the fireships that were now pushing through the entrance. The captain of the frigate Marty was shooting at compromised and detailed his marines to fire swivels and musket fire at the shore battery to try and disrupt them, while leaving the few main guns he had operational to try and sink the fireships.

There was an explosion and flames rose up in the town behind the harbour. The third team had gotten to work. Their mission was to locate and burn storerooms, magazines, armouries and anything that could be useful to the French Navy. They were also to try and stop the crew sleeping ashore returning to their ships.

Marty unslung his Durs Egg carbine from where it hung across his back and started sniping. The flames from the burning buildings conveniently outlined targets for him and the sun was coming up. He took out swivel gunners and targeted officers and anyone who looked like they were giving orders. At one hundred yards with a convenient wall to lean on and shelter behind, he could hardly miss.

The gun manned by Tom and the boys was reloaded first. They traversed it with handspikes so that the shot would hit at a slight angle to the hull and then loaded the red-hot shot at the last minute.

They fired and when the smoke cleared, they could see the odd shaped hole where the shot had entered.

Marty called over his shoulder.

"Bet you thought that would skip off!"

"Not at all!" laughed Tom

The second gun fired. The shot entered through a gun port hitting the barrel of the gun while it was pulled back for loading, sending two tons of iron spinning across the gun deck.

The corvette fire ship had entered the harbour. The crew had gotten off and were rowing away. The superstructure and rigging were consumed by flames, but her momentum carried her on. The xebec was stopped in the harbour mouth and sinking.

Marty held up his hand to stop the firing of the shore battery and beckoned the men forward to watch. The corvette glided across the harbour right into the big forty-gun frigate. Just as she reached it her guns started to go off as the flames reached the priming holes.

Flames jumped from the corvette to the frigate. Her crew tried to stop them, but the ship had been in harbour for weeks and her upper works were tinder dry. To make matters worse smoke was coming out of one the hatches near where the heated shot had entered. It took just a minute for them to decide that their best option was to abandon ship.

The other frigate was desperately trying to make sail to get away from the conflagration, but one thing about fire is, it pulls air into it. The draft of air being sucked into the huge fire was dragging the second frigate towards it. To seal their fate the xebec sank in the harbour mouth effectively closing it.

"You want us to target the brigantine?" Tom asked.

"Yes, finish the job properly," Marty replied.

The British left the island the same way they had arrived but left behind two burnt out frigates, a sunken brigantine and a lot of dead French sailors. There were casualties. The corvettes guns had been indiscriminate, and a ball had taken the lower left leg off a sailor from the Belle. There were several walking wounded and one death.

Chapter 5: News from home.

It was late 1801. Marty and Caroline were at a shipyard in Bombay checking over the construction of a fast transport. This ship was based on a Baltimore Clipper that Marty had seen smuggling contraband into France. It was designed with a sharp prow, raked stern, and three masts with hermaphrodite rig.

He had got them to make her deeper in the hull and slightly wider than a Baltimore Clipper but that would be countered by her extra length. Keeping her hydrodynamically efficient. The extra width and depth would make her more stable and give her more cargo capacity. The hull construction was well advanced, and Marty admired the lines. She looked fast even out of the water and would be three hundred and fifty-tons burthen, bigger by around fifty percent than a regular Baltimore Clipper.

She was designed to get their goods to Britain before anyone else. For convenience the Caroline would sail under the Company flag but in reality, she would be privately owned. If she worked out, then they would get several more built and create their own merchant fleet.

She was made of teak which made her slightly heavy and more expensive to make but she would be very durable. They would mount eight guns for 'last resort' protection, but she should be able to out sail anything else on the sea except maybe a Baltimore Clipper.

"She will be ready to launch in one more month, Sahib," the Indian architect who had designed her and was overseeing the build told them. "We will fit her masts and rigging once she is in the water and then you can take her for a sea test."

Back at their rented bungalow, they sat on the terrace with Marty's boys who had come along partly as protection but mainly because it gave them something to do and the new ship interested them.

"Will she be as fast as you hoped?" John Smith asked.

"She should be able to do the trip in ten to twelve weeks averaging twelve to fourteen knots," Marty replied. She won't carry a huge amount so we will only put valuable goods like tea and spices on her."

"We bin looking for crew and have twenty lined up and will have the full thirty soon." Tom reported.

"Captain Harrington will command her, and Charles Longstead will be first mate," Caroline added.

"He's out of America, isn't he?" Wilson chipped in.

"Yes, he was, but he was on the wrong side and had to leave straight after the war." Marty replied. "He is an aggressive sailor and will get the best out of her."

A shout and the patter of tiny feet announced the arrival of Beth. She was escorted by Blaez their Dutch Shepherd dog who had taken on the role of body guard for their energetic young daughter. Mary, their nanny, brought up the rear.

Marty swept her up into his arms and threw her up in the air, and Beth giggled happily as he caught her and swung her around.

Marty almost missed the look of surprise and concern on Tom's face and he turned his head to follow his gaze to see a man coming out of the bushes pointing a gun at them. Blaez had no hesitation. He charged forward, leaping off the terrace, sinking his teeth into the man's shoulder in mid leap and hung on. Momentum did the rest. Seventy pounds of dog traveling at close to twenty miles per hour has a lot of it and the man did a back flip before he hit the ground.

Marty thrust Beth into Mary's arms and was only beaten to the man by Matai who was trying to persuade Blaez to let him go, but Blaez wasn't interested, he had his teeth sunk well into his shoulder and was shaking him in anger. The man was howling and trying to hit the dog with his free hand but that just made him madder.

In the end Marty had to drag Blaez back by the collar after Matai used a trick he had learned while getting dogs to release their prey when he was hunting. He pushed his thumb into the gap behind the dog's teeth forcing him to open his jaws and let go.

As soon as he was free Tom and John held him by the arms and dragged him to his feet. Marty picked up the gun and checked it and was surprised to find it wasn't loaded.

They looked him over, he was European, around five feet four in height, sandy haired with blue eyes that were watering in pain. His left shoulder was bleeding, and Marty was sure there would be a fairly clear imprint of Blaez's teeth in his skin.

"Well, you got lucky my friend." Marty told him. "The dog got you before me and my friends filled you full of holes."

The man looked around and saw that every one of them held at least one pistol, including Caroline.

"Now why were you waving that pistol around?"

"I haven't eaten for three days," he sobbed in pain. "I found the pistol by someone who had been killed on a back street in the town so I thought I would try and get some money to buy food."

"By robbing us?" Caroline asked.

"Yes, biggest mistake of my life," he replied in tears, "but you were all sitting there looking well fed and" he looked around in disbelief "unarmed."

That caused a laugh and they all put their weapons away.

"What is your name?" Marty asked.

"Leon Ingridsson," he replied

"Swedish?"

"Yes."

"And that was the first time you'd tried to rob anybody?"

Leon looked at the floor.

"Yes, I am desperate."

"Let him go," Marty instructed.

Marty looked around, saw a couple of servants watching nervously and beckoned them over.

"Bring some food please. Samosas, pakoras, Bhajis and murgh makhani with bread for one person," he ordered. "and a bowl of warm water and some cloths."

When the water and cloths arrived, he asked Antton to see to his shoulder.

Antton sat Leon down at a table and gently started to work on his shoulder. Blaez had done a good job and he asked Mary to get him a large needle and some catgut from his room which he kept for stitching up bad cuts.

Mary put Beth down as she started to struggle and the little one ran over to Blaez and put her arms around his neck and gave him a big hug.

"Now why are you in Bombay and in such a mess?" Caroline asked.

"I was a topman on a merchantman, the Stockholm, and we had a really bad trip. When we got here, we were all given leave to have some shore time. I got drunk and was robbed while I was unconscious. When I came to and got back to the docks my ship had sailed."

He winced as Antton took a pocket flask of brandy from Wilson and poured it into the wounds.

"That was three days ago, and I haven't eaten since. I asked at ships, but they didn't need anyone. I don't know this town at all so didn't know where to go for help."

"There's no sailor's mission here yet," Tom observed.

The food arrived and before Leon started to wolf it down Antton put half a dozen stiches into his shoulder to close up the wounds Blaez's canines had caused. When that was done, and he was bound up he started to eat only slowing down when Caroline cautioned him not to make himself sick.

"You want a berth?" Marty asked

Leon nodded too busy eating to talk.

"You can have a berth on our new ship. You will be tested on the shake down voyage. If you shape up, we will keep you on. If not, then you will be put back on shore. Understood?" Marty said.

"I won't let you down sir," he replied

"Tom sign him on and give him some money for lodging and food."

After Ingridsson and Tom had left to get him a room at a cheap sailor's hostel near the docks Marty and Caroline settled down to open a pile of mail from home. They split them between them and sorted them into date order.

"The dairy is working out just fine and making its first profits," Caroline observed after reading a report from Mountjoy their Estate Manager. "The reorganisation of the tenancies into cooperatives has also been finished and apart from a couple of disputes seems to have settled down nicely. They started implementing your plans for crop rotation and land management . . ." she checked the date on the letter, "a year ago."

She opened a second letter from Mountjoy.

"Ha!" she smiled. "Crop yields are already up. Mountjoy attributes that directly to the soil improvements."

Marty smiled and then read out that:

"The agent has found two suitable farms in Dorset. They are next to each other and were owned by two brothers. Both died within six months of each other and neither had children."

"They had no children?" Caroline asked.

Marty read on for a minute then said.

"No, neither ever married. It used to be one farm. Oh, this is ripe! They were twins and the father damned them as a pair of sodomites in his will and split it between them on the condition they stayed single. If either married, they would both forfeit their inheritance. Seems the old boy didn't want them passing their proclivities on."

"There is a letter from your brother Alfred, what does he say about it?" Caroline said pointing at another letter in the pile.

Marty opened it and read it through.

"He says its prime land and the two farms together can make a fine estate. He thinks it would be best used for sheep on the hills and beef down in the valley with a bit of cereal for rotation. We should get Mountjoy to have a look and see what he thinks."

"He already has." Caroline was reading another letter. "He says Arthur asked him down and he agrees with him."

"I should have known." Marty smiled.

They worked their way through all the personal letters and then Marty opened one from Wickham. It was three months old, dated June 1801.

"They are still expecting Napoleon to sue for peace," Marty quoted. "The government is swallowing his overtures hook line and sinker. Wickham still thinks it won't last. He says we can stay here for a while if we want as Wellesley has indicated he might be able to use us."

"Trust Arthur to be thinking of himself," Caroline sighed she took a deep breath.

"Marty there is something you need to know."

"Yes darling," he replied without looking up.

"Dammit! will you pay attention?"

He looked at her quizzically.

She took another deep breath.

"I'm pregnant again."

The whoop Marty made as he swung her around in a hug could be heard over the whole house.

Chapter 6: What goes around.

The Caroline was ready for sea on time. She looked fast with her raked masts and streamlined hull. Marty and six of the boys were on board to see how she sailed. Caroline was suffering from morning sickness so decided to stay on shore. Christo and Matai stayed with her as security.

Captain Harrington was in command and Charles Longstead his First Mate. The crew were all experienced sailors and made up of Europeans and Indians. She had a full load of water and food for the crew but was empty of cargo and ballasted so she rode a little high in the water.

They cast off from the dock and warped her out into Mahim Bay. They set the staysail, and mizzen and she picked up the breeze immediately, headed out of the bay past Bandra Fort on the Northern point and out into the Arabian Sea.

There was a very stiff Easterly breeze once they got out to sea so they set the mainsail, jibs and topsails.

"She sails like a witch!" Marty whooped as they heeled over making better than ten knots.

They slowly increased the amount of sail she carried until they were carrying every stitch she could, and she was heeled over to the gunnels.

"She's fast alright," agreed Harrington, "but she is trimmed too far down at the bow and is griping a little. If we get her sat more on her heals, we could get another knot or two out of her."

"What about the rake?" Marty asked, "could she benefit from another couple of degrees?"

"Aye, we could try that too," agreed Harrington, "but let's get her trimmed right first."

They reduced sail and set the crew to work moving the water barrels and stores aft to lift the bow around a foot as she stood hove to. Once that was done, they set off again. The gripe was gone, and a cast of the log showed just under fifteen knots!

They decided that the masts could stay as they were and tried all the different combinations of sail they could. After three days they returned home.

Marty pronounced himself satisfied with the performance of their new ship and left the crew to take the slack out of the rigging caused by the new rope stretching and bedding in.

Marty and his men returned to their rented house and were met by an officer of the Bombay regiment at the gate. Marty was about to ask what was going on when Mary flew out of the house crying hysterically.

"They've killed poor Christo and took Lady Caroline and the baby!" she cried.

Marty froze for an instant then pushed past the officer and ran into the house followed by his men. The scene that met them was chaotic and there was ample evidence of a fight, Christo lay on the floor in a pool of blood. A bullet hole in his chest and his sightless eyes staring at the ceiling. Antton knelt and closed his eyes gently muttering something in Basque. There was also a dead Indian servant in the doorway to the drawing room and Garai saw to him with one of the Indian servants. Matai was nowhere to be seen.

Marty held up his hand and in an icy calm voice said, "I want every square inch of the house searched for clues. I want to know what happened and who did it. Don't move or touch anything until I have seen it."

He took Mary into the nursery, sat her down and asked her to tell him what she knew.

"It were early this morning before dawn. We was all asleep when Blaez started barking. Then I heard Matai and Christo yelling for Lady Caroline to lock her door. There was a shot and the sounds of a fight." She started to cry, and Marty hugged her and said softly.

"Shhh, take your time."

Mary took a deep breath and composed herself.

"I heard voices, then a banging like they were trying to break down a door. Then a crash and two more shots. Someone yelled and was swearing, and I heard Lady Caroline screaming."

She sobbed again.

"Then one comes into the nursery and Blaez he did go for him, but he was ready for that. He had a net or something and the dog jumped straight into the middle of it. He was all tangled up and the man gave him a right kicking. Then he comes over and took Beth. I tried to stop him, but he just punched me in the face."

She had the makings of a black eye to prove that.

"Did he say anything?"

"He told me I was only alive so I could tell you that you would hear when he was ready to name his terms for you to get your family back."

"English then?"

"Oh yes he were English."

"What did he look like?"

"A bit taller than you, solid built, brown hair, he had a scar on his forehead sort of curved like."

"Billy Smith," Marty snarled. "I should have killed him when I had the chance." He was blaming himself for what had happened but knew he had to control himself if he was going to help his beloved. He knew if he let guilt or doubt overcome him, he would be no use to his wife, child and unborn baby.

"Sir?" Mary asked wondering how he knew.

"I gave him that scar when we were ship's boys. I slammed his head in to the deck during a fight. There was a bolt head sticking up and it cut him."

Marty left her with a female servant and went to find Blaez. He was lying down in the drawing room on a blanket and, when Marty came in, he struggled to his feet and whined as Marty approached.

"Steady boy," he said as he knelt and ran his hands over his body. "Those bastards hurt you didn't they."

Blaez yelped as Marty brushed a rib and Marty felt another surge of anger.

"Cracked I reckon."

"Marty, we found some things you should look at," said Tom from the door.

Marty told Blaez to stay and went with Tom to their bedroom. Her pistols were on the floor. Both had been fired. There was smear of blood on the door. Tom pointed out more drops leading across to the bed and a torn sheet.

"Looks like she shot one of them," Tom observed, "and he tore a strip off the sheet to bandage it. They also ripped down the bell pull."

"Probably to tie her hands if she was fighting them," Marty concluded.

"From what we seen in the hallway and outside there were probably four or five of them," Tom continued and took Marty out to show him the evidence.

"There be two sets of bloody footprints where they trod in Christo's blood. See they be different sizes. Outside we found more prints and Garai says he can tell that four people made them."

"What happened to Matai?" Marty asked.

"Well there be more blood on the door frame by your study and whoever left it drew an M with a V on its side on the door."

"Let me see it."

The went to the door and Marty looked at the bloody marks.

"That's not a V it's an arrow," he decided. "Matai has left us a message."

He went into the study and carefully searched the desk, floor and shelves. There was nothing there. He stood back and looked again. Looking to see what wasn't there.

There was an empty space where he kept a jar with Blaez's treats.

There was a knock on the door and the officer who had been outside came in.

"My Lord, my men have secured the area around the house and the Bombay police have arrived. They would like to talk to you if possible."

A man in a bowler hat stepped into the room.

"Lord Candor? Detective Winter, Bombay police."

Marty just nodded to him, went over to his Arms Chest and unlocked it.

"I understand that your wife and child have been abducted. I wish to assure you that we will do everything in our power to find them and return them to you safely."

Marty took out his Durrs Egg Carbine and its ammunition, then his double-barrelled pistols. He placed them on the desk. Lastly, he removed his weapons harness and his hanger and put it on. He sat at the desk and started loading the pistols.

"I am very comforted to hear that Detective, but we have no time to waste and a trail we can follow," he looked at Tom.

"Get the boys ready to move out. I want them fully armed."

Tom nodded and left.

"Sir, I must protest," the policeman spluttered. "We need to do a proper investigation!"

"Well you do that," Marty growled as he clipped the loaded pistols to his cross belts and slung his knife on the left side of his belt. "You can catch up with us when you are done."

Marty stood and pushed past him. The Detective grabbed his arm.

"If you want to keep that you will let go now," Marty said very quietly and looked him in the eyes.

Detective Winter had never looked death in the face before and he was absolutely sure he never wanted to again.

Marty went into the drawing room and, crouching, talked to Blaez.

"Blaez my friend, I need you to find Matai for me. Can you do that?"

Blaez's ears perked up.

"Find Matai!" Marty commanded.

The dog pulled itself to its feet and headbutted Marty in the chest. Marty put him on his lead and stood up. Blaez walked slowly towards the door to the study and sniffed the blood on the floor and the door. His ears pricked up and he started to sniff the floor in the hallway.

The rest of the team were waiting outside the front door.

Blaez looked up and saw his pack stood around waiting for him. He knew what he had to do. He sorted through all the scents on the ground and homed in on Matai's. It was leading out through the gates and he kept his nose close to the ground and followed it. Just outside the gate he found one of his treats. He wolfed it down and got back on the scent. He noticed that Matai's scent was overlaid on the scent of the alpha female and the pup. He could also smell the stink of the one that had kicked him.

He followed and they came to a big road which a lot of people and animals had been travelling. It confused the scent and he started to circle. His chest hurt but not so bad as to make him want to stop. Then he got a hint of another treat. It was there! On the side of the road.

He wolfed that one down as well and picked up on Matai's scent again. It was following the wall up the road. He found a few spots of blood and licked them, tasting them. Not Matai. He followed the scent some more.

It turned down a side road. There was a treat on the corner. This was easier, there hadn't been so many people on this trail. He picked up the pace a little. The Alpha held him back keeping him to a walk.

He found another treat; the scent went into a narrow path between two buildings. He followed. He could smell The Alpha female stronger now, but Matai's was even fresher.

He had no sense of time or distance just the scent. He followed the narrow path until it came out into a bigger path and found another treat. Nice Matai, he could taste him on the treat. He cast around and the scent led down the hill towards the water. The scent became stronger and he led his Alpha to a wall and along behind it to where he knew Matai was sitting.

Marty saw Matai just as Blaez barked and pulled extra hard on his lead. He was propped against a wall and didn't look in a good way at all.

Tom and Antton went to him straight away and checked him over for wounds.

Matai's eyes opened and he grinned at Blaez.

"Knew you would find me boy," he said as the dog pushed at him with his head. Then he looked at Marty.

"They are in that boat out there in the estuary. The one with a single mast and cabin. I followed them after they left. They thought I was dead."

"You damn nearly were," Tom told him. "If this knife wound was half an inch to the left, he would have done fer you."

"Lucky me then," Matai smiled.

"You lead a merry chase." Detective Winter said as he puffed up to them.

Marty looked over the wall and assessed what he could see. Then he gave orders for someone to get a cart or a carriage to get Matai and Blaez back to the house.

He sat down with his back against the wall.

Winter made to say something, but Tom stopped him with a hand on his arm and a shake of the head.

Marty sat there, head back, eyes closed for close to ten minutes. His eyes opened and he looked around at the men he had available to him. It was enough.

"Detective," he opened, "your men have found a lead that the men who kidnapped my wife and child are hiding in a warehouse about two hundred yards over there. He pointed downstream. You will carry out a raid just after dusk on it today and make a lot of noise and start a fire."

"But we haven't . . ." he started to say when Tom leaned close and said.

"It's a diversion matey. The boss wants their eyes lookin' in that direction."

"Oh! I see."

"The rest of us will split into two groups and will approach the boat from upstream. The tide goes out at seven o'clock."

"Fishin' sculls?" John asked.

"Punts preferably, but anything that's really low to the water will do."

"On it!" replied Tom and disappeared around the corner dragging Garai with him.

"I want a constant watch set on that boat. I want to know how many are on there, when they take a piss and which ones are moving around."

A chorus of 'Aye aye skipper' came from the rest of the team.

Marty looked over at the Detective and said.

"Are you still here?"

As the sun went down and dusk settled over the estuary two dark shapes could be seen pull out from the shore a mile above where the kidnaper's boat was moored. They looked like typical Indian fisherman's rafts with a single man on the sculling oar at the stern. Each had a pile of nets and a single lantern suspended from a pole at the front.

As they got to a couple of hundred yards from the moored boat, there was the sound of a commotion on shore and shooting. As they drifted down on the current slowly closing on the bow, there was an explosion and a fire lit the sky. Three men came out of the cabin and stood at the stern rail and watched the flames. They didn't notice the rafts, or the lights go out.

Five shapes slipped over the bow. They wore dark clothes and their faces were blackened.

One of the men at the stern turned away from watching the fire and went forward to check the mooring rope. As he cleared the back of the cabin, he disappeared behind it with an odd jerky motion.

The larger of the two men looked around as if he heard something but then shrugged and went back to watching the fire.

Inside the cabin Caroline was sitting propped up on the single bunk with her young daughter in her arms. She had just got the youngster asleep when she heard a faint tapping on the bulkhead behind her head. She smiled as she tapped back.

"What was that?" asked the man who she identified as Stinky due to his aggressive body odour.

"What was what?" she asked back.

"That tapping."

"Death watch beetle," she replied.

There was a thud from outside the door and a splash.

Stinky grabbed a pistol and pointed it at her his eyes wide.

"Smithy! Smithy!" he called, "you all right out there?"

There was a groan from the other cot where the man she had shot as he entered her bedroom was laid out. She had shot him through the gut, and he was dying in terrible pain.

"He needs your help," she said, "he is in pain."

Stinky was obviously torn between going to find out what was going on outside and his friend.

"Look I will help him if you want to go and check outside. I can't get out there's only one door."

"Stay there," he said making up his mind.

He went to the door and stuck his head out. There was a crack and he fell to the floor.

The door opened and a familiar figure stuck his head around the jamb.

"Hello missus," he said.

"Hello husband," she replied. "Took your time."

"You weren't easy to find."

"Are Christo and Matai alright?"

"Matai will mend but Christo and one of the servants didn't make it."

Marty stepped over and took her in his arms as she started to weep.

She took a breath and asked.

"Did you kill the bastards who did this?"

"Not all of them. The leader and two," he looked down at the wounded one, "make that three will hang for it."

"Smith said he was doing this to get even with you. He said you ruined his life and he was going to ruin yours," she told him. "I think he planned to give you a ray of hope by asking for money to free me and then kill me anyway."

"Did he know you were pregnant?"

"Yes, he thought that was even better."

Chapter 7 No Good Deed

The judge had no hesitation in pronouncing sentence on the three survivors. The fourth died halfway through the trial.

William Smith, Reginald Cox and Fredrick Sloan were all sentenced to death for kidnap and the murders of Christo and the Indian servant. They would hang at dawn the next day.

By coincidence Arthur Wellesley had ridden into Bombay at the head of a brigade of cavalry the day before and he was present for the sentencing.

Marty, Caroline, Arthur and the boys were present the next morning to witness the sentence being carried out.

The official navy method was to hoist the condemned up by the neck, strangling the victim to death. That took about twenty minutes. The courts method was the short drop. The condemned was stood on a platform that was hinged at the back. The front was held up by a support that could be kicked away.

If they were lucky their neck broke and they died instantaneously, if not they strangled to death. It depended on how the knot was set. If it was set to the side, under the ear then there was a 50:50 chance of the neck breaking. However, if it was set at the back the neck would not break and they would strangle.

The three condemned were brought out, a priest walking with them. They were taken up to the platform and stood under individual hooks fixed to the ceiling.

Marty stepped forward.

"If the court will indulge me," he asked, "but I made a promise to Billy Smith."

"And what was that my Lord?" asked the judge who was overseeing the execution.

"That I would hang him myself if he crossed me."

The judge looked at the young man in front of him and saw determination in his eyes. He then looked at his wife.

She just looked back at him with no emotion on her face at all.

"Very well. It is irregular but there is no rule against it."

Marty took the steps up to the platform and walked over to Billy Smith.

"You should have gone back to Réunion when you had the chance," he said quietly as he slipped the noose over his head and tightened the knot, so it sat at the back of his head. "There," he said, "Navy style."

Billy said nothing. He was too frightened to speak.

When all three were fitted with their halters. Marty walked down the steps and picked up the rope that removed the support. He looked up at the judge who asked the men if they had any last words. They didn't.

He nodded to Marty who took a big breath and let it out slowly.

He took up the slack. *'For what you are about to receive I am eternally grateful.'*

He jerked the rope towards him, and the support came out from under the platform.

Billy Smith's bladder and bowels evacuated as he dropped, and he lost consciousness six and a half minutes later. He was pronounced dead twenty minutes after that. His co-conspirators fared no better.

Chapter 8: Pune

Matai and Blaez had recovered nicely from their wounds and the whole team were sat on the terrace of their bungalow enjoying the evening breeze.

It was early June 1802 and their new ship, The Caroline, had left with a cargo of top-quality tea and spices for Britain in January. She was on her way back with a cargo of fine wine and brandy. The sea trial of the new ship, an adaption of the Baltimore Clipper design, had gone so well they had commissioned two more from the same shipyard. The first was almost built and the keel of the second had been laid down.

Caroline was very close to term in her pregnancy and was increasingly bothered by the heat and snippy.

Marty was going through a pile of letters and newspapers that had arrived on the fast packet the evening before. A headline caught his eye and he unrolled the broadsheet to read it better.

"Good god, they've only gone and done it," he exclaimed to Caroline who was opening her letters and blurted out.

"They signed a peace treaty with Napoleon in March!"

"Really?" Caroline asked standing to look at the paper over his shoulder. Marty glanced at her, then at the rest of his team who were looking at him expectantly and put the paper on the table so all could read it if they were able.

The Treaty of Amiens, as it was called, was signed on March the twenty seventh by Britain, Spain, The Batavian Republic and France. It was lauded by the government spokesman as an historic act that would finally end the conflict between Britain and France.

"Bloody fool." Marty grunted.

Notable omissions in Marty's opinion were the lack of any reference to what would happen to Belgium, Savoy and

Switzerland or what would be the impact on trade with Europe.

France got back most of the territories they had lost during the war. *'So much for all the blood and sacrifice by the British military, bloody politicians.'* Marty thought.

Britain kept Trinidad and Ceylon. France would leave Naples and the Papal states. Egypt would be given back to the Ottoman Empire and Malta back to the Knights of Saint John.

There were other statements, but Marty was too depressed to read them.

"The politicians have sold us out," he sighed sadly and went back to reading the rest of his letters.

One from Hood cheered him up. He told him that the initial evidence was that Napoleon was using the peace to reform and rearm his army. The down side was that the politicians had ordered the Navy and Army to reduce their numbers, setting many experienced crews and soldiers on the streets with no work. Hood predicted the war would start again in a year.

A week later and Caroline went into labour. It was mercifully short, a matter of twenty hours and she only told Marty she hated him twice before he was unceremoniously kicked out of the bedroom so the midwife could do her work.

A hearty wail announced the arrival of the latest addition to the Stockley clan. James Charles Stockley had arrived. He weighed in at a healthy seven pounds.

Knowing that it would only be a matter of time before he was recalled Marty and Caroline agreed they needed to set up their trading and shipping business as soon as possible.

They set about interviewing people who could act as their agent and run their concerns in India. They chose a middle-aged Scott, Dougal McDonnel from Dumfries, who spoke softly but had evidenced real business acumen. He would source the cargos for the ships. Spices, Silks, precious stones and tea were all on his list.

He would be based in Bombay but would have a reach that covered the whole of India and would be free to recruit his own people. He would get a cut of the profits when the goods were sold in Britain and was very motivated.

They also employed a factor who would take care of the import and distribution of the fine wines and brandies that were sourced by the Deal Boys from France. The Deal operation had ceased smuggling and had turned into legitimate importers for the duration of the peace, but Marty knew they were ready and willing to revert to smuggling when the peace ended.

Setting up and establishing their import/export business kept them busy for most of the summer.

Arthur Wellesley, Governor of Seringapatam and Mysore visited with some news.

"Maharaja Holkar, who is not friendly towards the British, is preparing to attack Pune. He has rebelled against Daulet Rao Scindia who he calls a usurper and says he wants to free Peshwa Baji Rao from him. He has a point, as the Peshwa was put in power by the Maratha nobles led by Scindia and pretty much has to do what he is told," Arthur was telling him as Caroline entered the room.

"Holkar is already on the march with his army and is knocking over towns loyal to the Peshwa on his way. He is proclaiming his support for the Peshwa, but Baji Rao ordered the killing of Yashwant Rao's brother and is, understandably, not convinced Holkar has his good health at heart."

"Sensible man," Marty commented.

"Indeed, so the Peshwa has teamed up with Daulet Rao Scindia. It's a case of its better to ally yourself to the devil you know. They are going to face the Holkar's army at

Hadapsar around the twenty-fifth or twenty-sixth of October. I don't think they stand a chance.

"What do you want us to do?" Caroline asked.

"Now why would I want you to do anything?" he responded ingenuously with a sly smile.

"Arthur *you* don't just drop by for a social call and gossip," she observed sardonically.

Arthur laughed and responded.

"Touché my dear."

"So, what do you want me to do? You aren't telling me this for my entertainment mon amie," Marty smiled.

Caroline came over and sat on the arm of his chair and said coyly.

"Marty, what on earth would Arthur want from us! Why he has the might of the Empire and East India company to call on."

Arthur raised an eyebrow in amusement at the teasing and snorted a laugh.

"Well to be truthful we do have need of your special abilities."

He leaned forward.

"We need to get the Peshwa out from under the thumbs of the Lords so we can get him to sign a treaty with us."

"And he will be in his palace at Pune after the battle?"

"Yes, the Shaniwarwada. It's a vast place built in the last century and is the seat of the Peshwas. It's as much a fort as a palace. We expect them to lock the Peshwa up and hide the key once they lose to Holkar."

"If they do that we will know for sure where he is won't we," Marty observed and then asked. "Do we have the plans of the palace?"

"No, but Ranjit has spent quite a lot of time there and can give you a detailed briefing," Arthur responded.

"If we can get them to lock him in his rooms. I can slip him out and get a good head start back here to Bombay before they realize he is gone."

"What about the locks?"

Marty laughed.

"Locks are not a problem. I doubt they have a lock that can hold me up for more than a few seconds."

"Really? How do you do that?" Arthur asked intrigued. Caroline chuckled at his naivety, stood and went to a drawer in the dresser. She returned with a Joseph Bramah padlock that was purported to be the most secure every made. She closed and locked it, gave Arthur the key and the lock to Marty.

Marty took two probes made of steel from a pouch he had in the inside pocket of his jacket. Five seconds later the lock opened, and he handed it to Arthur.

"Good God! Nothing is safe!" he exclaimed. "Wickham told me in a letter that you and your team had 'special skills' but I never imagined . . . "

Marty laughed and said, "Arthur would it affect our friendship if I told you we were experts in everything needed to achieve any mission Wickham or Hood throw at us?"

Marty could see many thoughts and emotions pass across Arthur's face. He knew what those old devils were up to and, in many ways, it went against his instincts as a gentleman, but he was nothing if not a pragmatist, thought he knew the young couple in front of him and understood they were loyal to the core. In the end he sighed and looked first Marty and then Caroline in the eyes.

"You are the oddest pair I have ever come across. I know your heritage and how you came by your titles." He held up his hand as both opened their mouths to respond. "That doesn't bother me in the slightest, the damn aristocracy could do with an injection of new blood, but you keep surprising me with this other. . stuff. All I can say is – thank God you're on our side."

He grinned at them and added, "I don't suppose we could drink a glass of Madeira on that?"

The wine was promptly ordered, and Arthur stood and said, "I propose a toast. To friends with many talents!"

Two days later Marty was in his study with John Smith, Ranjit and Arthur. Ranjit was describing in as much detail as he could the layout of the Shaniwarwada, while John sketched it on a large sheet of paper. He had visited the main part of the palace many times and was able to describe the entrance and layout of the accommodation and entertainment wings. He had also visited the Peshwa in his rooms and had some idea about their layout and the route to them as well.

Marty had sent Antton and Garai on a scouting mission to Puna to check out the routes to and from the palace. Their information would be added to the map when they returned.

"Would they really lock the Peshwa in his rooms if you showed up unexpectedly?" Marty asked.

"If I claimed I was there to get his signature on a document they probably would. He would be suddenly indisposed or ill and unable to entertain visitors."

"Do the staff all wear uniform?"

"Yes, they do. The palace has its own special livery."

Caroline came in and sat in a chair. Blaez followed her as Beth was asleep in the nursery.

Arthur dug in his pocket and offered him a biscuit. Blaez gently took it out of his fingers without touching them.

"Here is another contradiction." Arthur said. "I have heard stories about this young fellow, about how much of a killer he is. But look at him!" Blaez had rolled on his back-inviting Arthur to scratch his tummy.

"He is just protective of his pack," Caroline observed and then smiled brightly and said. "I have some news.

Apparently the Peshwa will host a ball at the end of September and Lord and Lady Candor will be invited."

"Will he really," Arthur exclaimed, "and how do you know that?"

"Lady Mansfield heard it from Mrs Fotherington, who was asked who to invite by the Peshwa's private secretary. It will either be a celebration of his victory or an attempt to surround himself with allies after his defeat."

"Really. It seems I have been overlooking a valuable source of intelligence." Arthur wryly observed.

"Oh, you can just ask whenever you want to know what is going on." Caroline offered with a smile.

Ranjit looked up.

"They will lock him in his rooms after that for sure."

"And that opens up a host of possibilities," Marty smiled in satisfaction.

The time came for them to leave for Pune. It wouldn't be a long trip as Pune was around sixty miles Southwest of Bombay as the crow flies. They had a coach that Marty had bought two weeks before and had modified to suit their requirements. The team were dressed in new livery that Caroline had commissioned and rode as armed escorts. It had taken a bit of persuasion to get the boys to dress up, but once Marty had explained the plan, they had gone along with it.

The livery had a distinct Naval theme. Navy-blue military style long tailed jackets with silver double-breasted buttons over white shirts, blue cravats and snug white riding breeches. Hessian boots shined to perfection and French style Kepi hats.

If they were honest, they would have admitted they all looked rather smart. They all carried a musket, two saddle pistols, cutlasses and the usual hidden weaponry.

On top of the coach were a pair of servants and a driver in simpler and more Indian livery than the escort, all armed with blunderbusses that were hidden under their seats. Inside with

Marty and Caroline was Mary, the children's nurse, and the two children.

They took it easy and the horses walked rather than trotted so they only made forty miles the first day. They stopped in Lonavala in a house by the lake that was owned by a British Nabob.

When they pulled up at the palace in Pune, they had already heard that the joint forces of the Peshwa and Scindia had been roundly thrashed by Holkar. Holkar was resting his troops prior to marching on Pune proper.

Marty and Caroline allowed themselves to be guided into the palace and to their rooms. They were provided with servants but politely refused most of them saying that they preferred their own. They also insisted their escort was housed with them. They had timed their arrival to be around midday on the day of the ball, so they had half a day to settle in.

Marty dressed that evening to impress. He wore a high collared, deep blue, short tailed jacket that had solid gold buttons and delicate gold embroidery around the collar and cuffs. A fancy white silk shirt with a white cravat held by a gold pin with a stunning blue white diamond at its head. His sash of rank was a lighter blue with gold edging and held the gold and diamond coat of arms given him by the prince regent, his Order of the Bath and a single, solid gold bar to represent his lieutenancy.

Caroline was stunning in an emerald green silk ball gown that was cut low to show off her cleavage and clung to the figure that she had worked hard to get back after the birth of James. She wore a diamond tiara, diamond drop earrings and a necklace of diamonds with a huge emerald as the centrepiece which was matched by bracelets on her wrists. She carried a small handbag made of silver ringmail and wore a sash of matching blue with her diamond broach and a smaller Order of the Bath.

When they were announced there was an audible sigh from the gathered worthies. They looked the part and they played it to the hilt. Royalty couldn't have made a greater impression.

They moved through the room towards the Peshwa to pay their respects, the crowd parted and there were murmured greetings, which were returned. Some of the ladies curtsied and fluttered their fans at Marty. Caroline noted those who were particularly brazen.

They moved up to the Peshwa and the people who were talking with him immediately stood aside. He was a short man of only five feet two inches tall and of slight build. He had an impressive moustache and was dressed in a cloth of gold coat and trousers; his feet were encased in gold silk slippers. He was sat on a grand chair padded with cloth of gold covered cushions.

"Your Highness," Marty greeted him and bowed. Christine dipped a most elegant curtsey.

"Lord and Lady Candor!" he greeted them, smiling. "A most impressive entrance. I think the world stopped for a moment, stunned by your beauty Lady Caroline."

"You are too gracious your Highness." Caroline murmured.

"I was sorry to hear of your setback." Marty offered. "May I offer you a gift that may distract your Highness from your troubles and offer a modicum of comfort?"

Marty held out a cunningly devised golden rod, inset with precious stones. It was in fact a cleverly designed puzzle. Marty had heard that the Peshwa had a fascination for such things.

The little man's face lit up in a beaming smile as he took the gift from Marty's hand.

They talked for a few minutes more and then Marty and Caroline made way for the next couple to be introduced.

Marty noted that the Peshwa put his gift in his pocket rather than pass it to the servant that was hovering nearby. He smiled.

The ball went the way many balls do, and they danced, socialized and networked as well as ate and drank. It came to an end at one in the morning when they retired to their rooms.

At three AM the palace was silent and a pair of figures dressed in palace livery and carrying a tray of drinks walked through the corridors. They glided past sleeping servants who were stationed outside of guest's doors and made their way to a part of the palace off limits to visitors.

They walked past soldiers stationed in the corridors until they came to the door they were searching for. There were a pair of guards and the servants offered them the refreshments. The guards drank and then almost together slumped quietly to the floor. One of the servants knelt at the lock and inserted a pair of metal probes. Seconds later he quietly opened the door.

The guards down the corridors saw two servants returning carrying a tray with empty glasses.

The next morning at eight o'clock the palace was in uproar. The Peshwa was missing! The word was that his private rooms had been infiltrated and he had been spirited away through a window, down a rope and through the gardens.

The guest's rooms were checked but they found nothing. Search parties were sent out and they even had dogs tracking the scent of the Peshwa across the grounds and out into the countryside.

Then they got word that Holkar was on the move, which prompted a general mobilisation, so Marty and Caroline gathered up their luggage and their people and left along with all the other guests.

In the throne room Scindia fumed and raged. Not only had the Peshwa disappeared but Holkar was coming and he had nowhere to run.

Once they had cleared the city limits of Pune and they were safely on the way to Bombay the coach stopped by a copse of trees. They got out and Tom got in and removed a cleverly disguised section of the back seat. It revealed a hidden compartment just big enough to sit a single person comfortably.

The Peshwa stepped out a little stiffly as he had been in there for around six hours. He looked around then grinned at Marty.

"A most excellent plan Martin. Scindia's dogs are all running in the opposite direction?"

"Yes, our man will lead them a merry chase."

"Hiding a message inside the puzzle rod was very clever. I suppose my fascination for puzzle objects made it inevitable that I would find it."

Marty smiled and said.

"It was a gamble, but the odds were good once I saw you put it into in your pocket."

Marty had the rod especially made at quite some expense. It was a genuine puzzle that had been dressed up with gold plate and coloured glass to make it look expensive. Marty had gambled that once the Peshwa saw what it really was he would twig that it was other than just an amusing gift.

One of their escort moved over and bowed to the Peshwa.

"Gupta you are a loyal and faithful servant and I thank you for helping me. You look good in the uniform of Lord Candor's guards, but better in your own clothes," the Peshwa said to him.

Gupta bowed again and went to get changed. He had taken the place of Matai, who was laying the false trail, so the palace guards wouldn't notice a change in their numbers. He had sacrificed his moustaches and had to wear makeup to lighten his skin, but as Marty had said during the planning, "to the guards our escort probably all look alike so we should get away with it."

They had something to drink and the Peshwa changed into European clothes for the rest of the journey.

Newly confirmed Major General, Arthur Wellesley and Marty sat around a large table in Fort Bassein with Peshwa Baji Rao and General Lake. There was an ornate document on the table between them. From it hung the seals of the Governor General of India and the Peshwa of Maratha. Both men had signed it thus confirming the Bassein Accord, a treaty between the Maratha Empire and the British. It was the thirty first of December 1802.

General Lake looked around the table.

"History will note this day as one which saw the course of Indian British relations take a momentous step forward. However, history will not record the efforts of Martin and his people to achieve this. So, I want to voice our thanks and appreciation to him here and now."

Peshwa Baji Rao stood, stepped over to a side table and returned with an ornate chest that was around a foot by nine inches at the base and nine inches high.

He placed it in front of Marty and said.

"Please accept this as a token of my gratitude. Without your help I would be a prisoner of Holkar or more likely dead." He opened the lid and inside on velvet cushions were two four-inch-long, exquisitely made golden tigers with ruby eyes and diamonds for claws. They were surrounded by seven large sapphires.

"The Tigers represent you and Lady Caroline. If you look carefully you can see one is a male and the other female. The sapphires are for your men."

"You are more than generous, and I thank you for myself, my wife and my men." Marty said sincerely as he examined the extremely fine work that had gone into making the tigers. They were priceless in his estimation.

Chapter 9: Ceylon

Marty and Caroline decided to return to Madras using one of their new ships. She was the second one built and was called The Bethany after their daughter. They had taken on a new captain, Phillip Tarrant, who had sailed into Bombay in a merchantman that had been heavily mauled by a storm in the Indian Ocean. The simple fact he had gotten the floating wreck into port at all spoke volumes about his seamanship. Added to that, he had also brought most of his crew and his cargo back intact as well which made him very attractive to Marty.

Tarrant brought his crew and his first mate with him. They recruited some twenty new men and they were ready to go.

As a cargo ship The Bethany actually made a comfortable yacht. They had fitted her out with temporary cabins which were very comfortable and could accommodate the entire team plus servants.

Mary had her hands full with the two children. Two-year-old Bethany was full of mischief and would disappear on her adventures as soon as Mary took her eyes off her. Young James was demanding and seemed to be always hungry, which kept Caroline busy. Blaez was never far away from either of them.

They sailed South from Bombay down the West coast of India past Goa, Mahé and Cochin and decided to spend a day or two in Ceylon.

They sailed into the harbour of Colombo and the first thing they saw was the huge fort positioned on the entrance to the harbour. Then, as they slowly made their way into their holding ground, they could see that much of the land around the harbour was given over to commercial buildings where they could see all manner of goods being traded and manufactured.

They spent the night onboard and first thing in the morning Marty went ashore to talk to the port authority about visiting the Governor.

The harbour master turned out to be a Dutchman, which shouldn't have been surprising as Ceylon was a former Dutch colony. Martyn van Boxtel was a naturally cheerful man with a round face and shining brown eyes. He did however express some concern about them coming ashore let alone visiting the Governor, who was in a temporary residence in Kandy to be closer to the King.

"There is a quiet rebellion going on. There is still some resistance to British rule and Governor North has had to clamp down hard in some areas."

Marty explained to him that he had an 'escort' and that they were all experienced military men. Eventually Van Boxtel reluctantly agreed to find him a carriage and riding horses so that they could travel to Kandy.

On returning to The Bethany, Marty gave instructions to the team to prepare for travel. He wanted them all armed with pistols and muskets as well as cutlasses.

He changed into travel clothes and donned his weapons harness. Two double barrelled pistols, knife and hanger, stilettoes in forearm sheaths and his lace up boots with their hidden blade and lockpicks. He slung his Durs Egg carbine over his shoulder and its ammunition and powder in a bag to hang from the saddle.

Caroline wore a simple dress with boots. She had her small pistols in pockets in the dress and had knives in both boots. When Marty raised an eyebrow at that she said something about what was good for the gander was good for the goose. He didn't know about the third, small double-barrelled pistol she had strapped to her thigh.

"Anyone would think we were going to war not for a visit to the governor." Marty laughed as he looked over his party.

They rowed ashore when the open landau style carriage and horses turned up on the dock. Van Boxtel looked impressed when they came ashore and efficiently organised themselves and the servants.

Caroline, Mary and the children rode in the carriage with two servants and the luggage. The men all rode horses and they set out in formation with Marty, Blaez, Tom and John at the front and the Basques bringing up the rear.

They rode out of Colombo and headed up the road, well track really, towards Kandy. They had been moving along nicely, as the dirt road was reasonably flat and only mildly rutted, when Franco rode up beside Marty and said.

"We are being watched," he inclined his head. "The hill to the west."

Marty casually looked around sweeping the horizon and spotted a figure squatting on the top of the hill. He was dressed in Indian clothes and had a long musket held upright beside him.

"Got him. Drop back and keep an eye on him."

Marty dropped back beside the carriage and leaning over in the saddle he warned Caroline about their shadow. She surprised him when she informed him, smugly, that she had not only spotted that one but there had been another on a hill as they left Colombo.

Marty went back to his position at the head of the column muttering about smart mouthed women.

Their shadows did nothing more than just watched, moving from hill top to hill top, so they stopped at the halfway point and set up their picnic for lunch. The men kept their guns close to hand and their eyes open.

They packed up after an hour and started out again moving higher as the road made its way up into the hills. They became more alert as the terrain got rougher and more suitable for someone to set an ambush.

The road skirted a hill with an almost sheer drop on the right and a wooded slope on their left. Marty heard Blaez growl and saw his hackles come up as they approached a corner, so held up his hand to signal everyone to stop. He unslung his carbine and that signalled the others to do likewise. There was a series of clicks as hammers were drawn back to half cock.

Blaez had his attention fixed on the road ahead. He was focused, his eyes and ears ahead and his right foot raised. He growled again.

Marty's horse shifted, picking up on the tension. Marty dismounted and signalled to the others to wait. He walked slowly forward and Blaez kept pace when he suddenly lowered his shoulders and head, so they were level and raised his hackles. He looked exactly like a wolf.

Marty stopped, pulled the hammer on his carbine back to full lock and checked the priming. Taking one quiet step at a time he and Blaez moved forward to the apex of the corner. As soon as he could see ahead without revealing himself, he knew what Blaez was warning him about. There was a tree across the road with half a dozen armed men behind it.

He checked the forest to the side and couldn't see anything but would put money on there being more men hidden in there.

He walked back to his horse, the carriage and his men.

"There is a roadblock with half a dozen men armed with muskets blocking the road. I would lay odds that there is at least another half dozen in the trees."

Antton looked around at the hills and then at the other Basques.

"Looks just like home," he grinned and said something to the others in Basque.

They slipped off their horses and tying them to the back of the carriage, melted into the trees.

After ten minutes Marty grinned and said, "let's go spring the trap."

They walked forward. Marty started to whistle a shanty.

They rounded the corner and the men behind the tree brought their guns to bear. Marty stopped and faced them. He appeared totally at ease and kept his carbine laid across his lap.

An arrogant looking man in a dirty coat stood up and pointed his gun at him. Marty just waited. The man looked slightly confused by the lack of reaction and shouted something in, what Marty assumed, was the local language. He just shook his head and shrugged pointing to his ear to show he didn't understand.

The man shouted something at him and gesticulated with his gun. Marty was going to shrug again when Blaez lost patience and launched himself forward snarling.

Marty didn't hesitate as Blaez distracted the men with his charge. He brought his gun to his shoulder, shot the leader in the chest and kicked his horse forward. He held the carbine in his left hand with his reins and pulled one of his pistols.

Tom had come up beside him and was firing his musket. John was on the other side and fired his. Two more men dropped and a third was screaming as Blaez ripped into his armpit.

There was a boom from behind them and Marty spun in the saddle to see the body of an ambusher fall back into the treeline. He was surprised to see Mary stood in the landau with a smoking blunderbuss pistol in her hands.

The remaining men from the barricade were running for their lives down the road when Antton stepped out of the trees to the side with a bloody knife in his hands.

Marty rode back to the carriage and looked at Mary who was wide eyed and pale. He leant over and gently took the gun from her hands. She looked at him her mouth formed an O and she sat back onto the seat with a thump.

Caroline put her arms around her and looked at Marty with a look of amazement on her face. Beth started to cry, and Mary leaned forward to pick her up and comfort her.

Marty got Antton to check the body and he reported that whoever he was had taken the full load in the centre of the chest.

"He must have been moving before we got behind them. There are another four back there."

"All dead?"

"Yes."

"Get that tree moved and let's get moving again."

He examined the blunderbuss which was, to all intents and purposes, a small hand cannon. It was made of brass, looked to be British made for the postal service and weighed a good six pounds. He just wondered where Mary had hidden it as he had never seen it before.

As he always said an unloaded gun was just a club, he reloaded it with four normal pistol balls and gave it to Caroline.

Mary seemed to have regained her composure by the time the road was clear, and the boys brought the bleeding survivor to him. Blaez had made a real mess of his armpit.

"The Governor may want to question him so we will take him with us. Wrap his wound and put him in the carriage. Caroline," he started to say but Caroline had already produced a pistol and laid it on her lap stopping him in mid-sentence.

Caroline asked Mary where she had gotten the blunderbuss pistol from.

"My brother got it for me before we left England. He works for the postal service and said that even I couldn't miss with this," she told her. "I will never forgive myself for not using it when you and the babe were kidnapped in Bombay so when he came out of the woods I just . . . ."

"Where did you hide it?" Caroline asked.

"I made a pouch for it under the baby's cot but when we travel, I put it in this compartment on the side of my travel bag." She opened a compartment on the side of the bag she carried the children's spare nappies and clothes in and put the gun in. When it was closed you would never know it was there.

They pulled up at the Governor's residence just before dark and were met by a flustered Major Domo who had not expected visitors let alone someone of obvious importance with an escort and a prisoner.

The Governor appeared. He was dressed in a smoking jacket and silk slippers and approached Marty.

"Who the devil are you sir?" he asked agitated by the unexpected intrusion.

Marty gave him his most urbane smile and replied.

"Governor North I presume," he said and held out his hand. "Martin Stockley, Baron Candor, at your service."

Caroline joined him at his side, and he continued.

"My wife, Lady Caroline. Sorry to impose on you but we had a slight delay on the way up here. Some fellows tried to ambush us. That one over there is one of the survivors."

The Governor looked from him to Caroline, to the team and finally at their prisoner. He opened his mouth to say something when a lady appeared in the doorway and said.

"Frederick! Why are you keeping our guests waiting out here?" She bustled over to Caroline and said. "Come in my dear and bring the children with you." She looked at Mary who was still a little grey. "Oh, my dear you look as if you have had a terrible shock. Come in come in!" and she shepherded the women and children through the front door.

Frederick looked bemused but pulled himself together and said.

"Well I suppose you had better come in as well." Turning to his Major Domo he ordered.

"Get the guard to put that fellow in the cellar for the time being and make these men comfortable in the barracks. Then prepare rooms for Lord and Lady Candor and their family." Turning back to Marty he said.

"Well come on then," he looked down at Blaez, "is that beast with you?"

The ladies and children went to the drawing room and Marty and Frederick went to the library.

"Now you better tell me everything including why you are here and why I got no warning."

Marty filled him in on why they were in India and their journey from Colombo.

"I know van Gerwin sent a messenger to warn you we were coming. I can only assume he was ambushed by the same men who tried it on with us."

"Bigger fools them then." Frederick observed. "Do you always travel so well . . . equipped?" he asked looking at the weapons laid out on the table where Marty had placed the visible ones.

"In our line of work its best to be prepared," smiled Marty which caused a speculative look to cross Frederick's face.

"We had better join the women. Martha will have organised the household to accommodate you by now. Best to stay out of the way when she is in organising mode or she tends to sweep you up in it." The Governor said with a man to man knowing look. "You can leave your . . . things, there. Sandri will make sure they're taken to your room."

They joined the ladies in time to have a glass of wine before they were called to dinner. Mary had recovered her composure due more to the motherliness of Lady North than anything else. The children were fast asleep with Blaez settled down near them.

They ate a surprisingly well prepared five course meal, considering the short notice that the kitchen had been given.

After dinner, the men sat in the library with Frederick. He smoked a cheroot while they drank port and discussed the politics of the region.

"Sri Vikrama Rajasinha is the 'King' or 'Raja' and he is the titular head of the Buddhist religion here and is the only block to us taking total control of the island," he explained. "We are in cahoots with the first Adigar, Pilimatalauwa, to provoke the King into an open act of aggression that we can use as an excuse to take over the Kingdom. It is a long game and may take a while to come to fruition."

"These minor acts of rebellion are a by-product of that?" Marty asked.

"Yes, and we will have to move this household back to Colombo soon as it is getting too dangerous to keep it here," the governor sighed.

"What about the gem mines? Are they under our control or the King's?" Marty asked.

"Interesting point that," Frederick replied thoughtfully. "The mines are in the highlands which are largely under the King's rule, but the traders are all in the coastal region under our control. Are you interested in gems?"

"We are setting up our own merchant fleet under the auspices of the East India Company and will be exporting high value cargo's by fast ship to Britain and importing wine and brandy to India on the return trips," Marty told him. "We have appointed agents in Bombay and Madras to source spices, gems, silks and the like and are setting up distribution for the wines and spirits."

"Very wise," Frederick agreed. "Would be interested in sending back the odd shipment myself," he added, with a sideways look to Marty, who nodded. "The Europeans will pay premium prices for good wine and spirits, but I have to ask what a Lord of the Realm is doing getting involved in trade?" Marty laughed and told him the truth of their backgrounds. It gave Frederick something to think about.

In the morning they interrogated their prisoner, but he would only say he was following the man Marty shot and that they were just there to rob European travellers. Frederick decided that they should hand him over to the local justice system as hanging him themselves would be inflammatory.

They decided to spend a few days in Kandi and were shown the Temple of the Tooth which housed the relic of the tooth of the Buddha. It was a tradition that whoever held the tooth would rule the country, which explained the importance of Kandy in the political landscape. Marty joked that maybe they should steal the tooth. Frederick didn't see the funny side of that comment and told him firmly that would send the whole island up in flames.

They noticed that they were followed everywhere they went. The boys were on high alert and carried their weapons conspicuously. At one point a man approached them, shouting something in Tamil at Marty and then at the ladies. He shook his fists and was getting increasingly agitated. Tom intervened, stepping up to him. He towered over the man and kept walking forward forcing him backwards. He didn't put a hand on a weapon nor raise a hand threateningly just walked forward. The man soon realised he was looking foolish as he ranted and walked backwards at the same time. When he tripped on a pile of cow shit and ended up on his backside, the incident ended.

Over breakfast the next morning Frederick was interrupted by a messenger. He returned to the table with a troubled look.

"We have had notice to leave Kandy," he announced. "The Adigar has sent warning that there will be a spontaneous demonstration that will result in them storming the residence."

"How long have we got?" his wife asked perfectly calmly.

"He says that the demonstration will start after prayers on Friday," he replied.

Martha rang a bell and the Major Domo came in.

"Sandri, please tell the staff to start packing we are moving back to Colombo."

Sandri bowed and calmly left the room as if this happened every day.

Seeing Marty and Caroline's puzzled expressions she clarified.

"We have a contingency plan in place for just this occasion. As the tension has increased, we have made sure we have pre-packed everything that isn't in everyday use and the staff have packing cases and materials ready for the rest.

"We also have carts and oxen ready for an evacuation. To be honest we have been expecting this for a couple of months now."

"We will join you then," offered Marty. "Our weapons and men may be needed."

"They will certainly help," Frederick admitted. "We only have a section of mounted sepoys as an escort." He thought for a moment, "I think we should leave first thing tomorrow."

Dawn the next day saw the entire household fed and ready to leave. The courtyard of the house was full of four wheeled oxcarts, two carriages and eighteen riding horses. The gates were opened, and four sepoys led them out, followed by four oxcarts, then the two carriages and last two more oxcarts. Four more sepoys brought up the rear, they were armed with lances and carried muskets slung across their backs.

Marty and his men ranged along either side and the sergeant of the sepoys rode beside the Governor's carriage. Marty suddenly signalled and he and his men left the column of carts and headed towards the palace.

They had made a fair amount of noise as they moved out and had a mile or more of the town to get through before they got to the open countryside. Word of their departure made its way rapidly to the palace and a mobilisation of fifty or so 'demonstrators' was organised. The mob made its way rapidly towards the outskirts of town to try and cut off their escape.

They got about half a mile when they came upon a barricade of carts, wooden crates and boxes stacked across the road between two houses. Behind it were eight men armed with muskets. A volley was fired above the mob's heads and they came to a stop. A man came to the front of the mob and waved a sword above his head as he harangued the crowd. There was another shot impossibly soon after the first volley and the man clutched his leg as he fell to the floor.

The mob milled around not sure what to do, wasting precious minutes. Two shots were heard in the distance and the barricade suddenly caught fire. It was soaked in oil and went up with an impressive WOOSH! The men behind it retreated to horses they had tied up thirty yards behind them. A last volley of shots rang in the air as they galloped away and a cry of,

"YEY, YEY, YEY, YEYAGH!" was heard.

With the slow carts it would take them two days to get to Colombo and they made a very nervous camp that night. There were two guards on watch at all times positioned outside of the camp with their backs to the fire to preserve their night vision. Marty had one of his men and a sepoy share the watch for two hours and then they were replaced. That way everyone got some sleep by the time they left again at dawn.

Marty rode beside the Landau and chatted to Caroline.

"There was a lot of smoke coming from Kandy when you got back to us" she observed.

"Yes, well I forgot most of their houses are wooden with stucco so our little fire may have gotten out of hand," he replied wryly, "but it bought us the time we needed to get away."

Caroline laughed and said, "well Mary and her cannon don't need any more excitement, so I guess it's alright then."

They eventually made it into Colombo without any further excitement and rolled into the Governor's residence to be met by his staff. Martha had them all installed, and a decent meal served by suppertime.

The next day Marty discussed gems with Frederick, and he sent a message to a trader he knew quite well. The man was a Ceylonese. Short like all of them with a bustling manner, his name was Priah Mudaliar. He maintained he was the most successful dealer in gems on the island and produced a pouch with samples for Marty to look at.

"I am afraid I am not the expert in gems," Marty admitted. "I will ask my wife to join us if you don't mind."

Caroline came to join them, and the trader was most solicitous but a little confused that a woman was being involved. She checked each gem against the daylight from the window and even used a small magnifying glass to check their clarity. Satisfied she leant back in her chair and said.

"These stones are of good quality, but can you supply more of the same?"

"How many would you like?" he replied thinking this woman would just want enough to make a necklace.

"As many as you can get. We want to be your exclusive exporter. We will take all types as long as they are of the first quality and cut," she stated calmly. "We will pay the asking price and you take your profit from that."

His eyes were alight with greed as he agreed.

"These stupid British don't know what the asking price is, I can skin them alive," he thought. Then he looked at the young man.

"I wouldn't think you can rob us if I were you," Marty said looking him in the eyes. "Our factor is well aware of the asking price for the gems and if you try and hike the price we will know."

He smiled and Priah's blood ran cold.

The Bethany left for Madras the next day.

Chapter 10: Return to Duty

They arrived back in Madras and resumed life in their bungalow. There was a pile of mail waiting for them and one was from the Admiralty. It was from Lord Hood and was addressed to Lieutenant Stockley. After the usual preamble it basically told him to get back to England as soon as possible and to report to the Admiralty for further orders. It was dated November twenty-second, 1802 and had taken over four months to reach him as it was now mid-February 1803.

Caroline was happy. She had been feeling homesick for a while now and they had set up all the business opportunities they wanted to. So, the house was packed in record time and they boarded The Bethany.

They had a cargo of spices and gems on board so despite using most of the cargo space for accommodation they would still net a good profit from the voyage. Caroline had informed their Factor and Agent in Madras about the arrangement with Mudaliar in Ceylon and she had bought everything of quality he had in stock.

Marty wrote to Arthur and General Lake thanking them for their hospitality in India and informing them of his recall. He made sure all the servants got an excellent leaving present except the two that were going home with them. Then he realised that his time here was done. He sent the letters ashore and commanded the captain to set sail. If all went well, they would be back in England in three months.

They were at the end of the dry season, so the winds were from the Northeast and The Bethany flew Southwest under a billowing cloud of white sails. This was the first time that Caroline had experienced one of their clippers sailing to the best of her capabilities and she found it exhilarating. They were stood on the foredeck watching a pod of dolphins racing their bow wave with Bethany.

Tom was standing by the foremast and John joined him. They stood and watched the happy couple for a while.

"They be turning out alright considering," John observed.

"Considering what?" Tom asked quizzically.

"Well 'is background and her being older and that," John replied.

"What yer on about?" Tom snapped back annoyed. "What difference do a couple of years make? They be the most well-matched pair I ever saw."

"Yes, but he be from . . ." he looked at Tom and realised that whatever point he was trying to make was being missed by a country mile and gave up.

"Oh, never mind," he grumbled.

Tom clapped him on the shoulder and laughed.

"Let's go and have a wet."

They didn't stop at Cape Town but passed it on Marty's birthday. He was twenty-two years old, married to the love of his life, had two wonderful children and was as rich as Croesus and getting richer. Things couldn't get any better.

Turning Northwest out into the South Atlantic they beat against a contrary wind until they picked up the South-easterly trade and ran with it up towards Brazil. Then North, up through the Caribbean, stopping at Trinidad to re-water and get fresh supplies, and on to the Carolina's where they could pick up the Northwest trade and head for home.

Liverpool was the target of their homecoming and they rode out several severe winter storms before they entered the Irish sea from the South and made their way up to the Mersey estuary. It was the second week in May, they had done the trip in three months.

Liverpool was loud, smelly, busy and generally unpleasant. They rented a carriage at an inflated price and at the very first opportunity headed down to their home in Cheshire.

In denial of his orders, Marty took a week to catch up on things domestic and the state of the estate. He was generally satisfied as Mountjoy had done an excellent job both in Cheshire and on the new lands in Dorset. Then, calculating he had pushed his goodwill with the Admiral to the limit, they headed down to their London house.

Tom and the boys complained about the cold incessantly during the trip. They had become very accustomed to the warmth in India and even travelling inside a coach with extra blankets didn't help that much. Marty knew how they felt but couldn't resist having the odd jibe at their expense.

Marty reported to the Admiralty on the tenth of May 1803 in a uniform that felt strange, and only had to wait an hour in the dreaded waiting room before being called to Admiral Lord Hood's office. He was looked at curiously as the Indian sun had turned his complexion a nutty brown, which stood out against the pallid white skin of the locals.

He entered the familiar office and saw his elderly mentor sitting at his desk. He looked no older than he had when he saw him before he left. If anything, he had put on a little weight.

"Martin my boy! So good to see you again." Hood greeted him warmly. "Just in time too as I expect peace to end any day now."

Mart sat in surprise at the news.

Hood laughed.

"Armand and Linette are in France and are sending back weekly reports. Your smugglers will be back to their regular business soon."

"And the S.O.F.?" Marty asked.

"That is why you are here." Hood stated with the emphasis on the 'that'. "You are to take command of the Flotilla."

Marty felt a sudden nervousness; he had been off of a deck for too long.

"We want it fully operational and expanded with a task force of marines for amphibious landings."

"Our targets?" Marty asked.

"Anything in range of the coast wherever you can cause most aggravation, disruption or consternation down to the Spanish border."

"Poof! That's a hell of an ask with all due respect Sir."

"And one you are more than capable of managing," Hood laughed. "Your holiday is over. Oh, and by the way Arthur Wellesley is very impressed with your abilities. You have gained a valuable supporter there as that young man is destined for great things."

Mart smiled at the thought of reacquainting himself with the mercurial general.

"Nelson also mentioned you as well. Thought you were a renegade but a 'damn useful one'."

"Now I advise you get yourself back down to Deal. Campbell will be your number two and have command of The Snipe. If you need any more ships, then you had better steal them as the damn politicians are still in denial."

Marty stood and bowed.

"Can I say I've missed you Sir?" he said with some affection. "India was fun, but you and Mr Wickham always add a bit more spice to life."

Hood laughed and waved him away. After he left, he sat and thought *'Damn if the boy isn't just like a son!'*

Marty visited the de Marchets' with Caroline and the children. They hadn't gone back to France during the peace except for one short visit to see what was left of their home. Disappointed and disgusted at the ruins of what remained they returned to England.

"The revolution destroyed everything of beauty," the Countess told Caroline sadly. "What they couldn't steal they destroyed or befouled."

Their son, Antoine, had signed up as a midshipman and was currently serving on the seventy-four-gun, third rate, HMS Albion under Captain John Ferrier.

Contessa Evelyn, their daughter and one-time childhood love of Marty, was married to her soldier boy, Arthur Simmonds, who was now a Captain in the Life Guards. They had a son of their own, Guillaume and had a house near Horse Guards. As soon as they received a message that Marty and Caroline were there, they came around to visit. Beth and Gui got on famously and happily played as the adults talked. Young James amused himself with Blaez until Caroline took the bone, they were trying to share, away from both of them.

He arrived at the farm on the eighteenth of May, which was coincidentally the day that Britain declared war on Napoleon again for not leaving the low countries. The boys and Blaez immediately made themselves at home, taking up where they had left off.

The Alouette was in great shape having been recently refit but The Lark was showing her age. James Campbell was the senior mid and was showing great maturity. Ryan Thompson also had an impressive record but lacked Campbell's initiative and made a good number two.

Many of the same men were there and Bill was still in charge of the Deal boys. Marty felt at home.

He was just getting his feet back under the table when a new contingent of forty Marines arrived. His old friend Paul La Pierre, who had been the lieutenant of marines on The Falcon, was in command.

"How on earth did you get this detail?" Marty asked. "Did you get caught with the Admiral's daughter?"

La Pierre laughed and explained that the Falcon had been a victim of the politician's peace dividend and had been put into ordinary. He had been on the beach for almost a year when Admiral hood asked him to command the marines in a 'special unit.' He jumped at the chance. It wasn't until he received his written orders that he found out that Marty was the commanding officer.

"Oh, so the old fox knew we had worked together before then," Marty laughed.

Chapter 11: Reformation

Marty and James sat together with Paul and discussed what they needed to deliver amphibious forces rapidly onto beaches in enemy territory. They weren't going to start a war. They needed to get ashore move inland, destroy their target and get the hell out of there. They had sixty marines and some sailors who could be effective as a raiding force.

In typical fashion they got all the core team together and discussed it in an open session.

"Who has been the best at this in history?" asked John Smith surprising everyone.

"Well the Romans, Normans and the Vikings," replied Ryan Thompson who, it turned out, was a closet scholar.

"An' what sort of boats did they use?" John Smith persisted.

"Well, the Vikings used long boats. Shallow draft boats that could be sailed or rowed as needed. They had a low enough freeboard that they could jump over the side and get ashore fast. They sailed those from Norway to England. The Romans used galleys."

"Well then, it's simple, we needs some of them long boats," John stated.

"Where we goin' to get them from then?" Tom asked.

James Campbell had been looking thoughtful. "We make them," he said

"What?" said Marty.

"We make them. Or rather we get our friends the shipwrights along this estuary to make them based on the design of a whaleboat." James continued.

"A whaleboat?" Marty asked unfamiliar with the design.

"Same basic shape as a Viking longboat only smaller. You can carry ten men with light equipment in one, plus the rowers. They are very seaworthy and are double ended so you don't have to turn them around on the beach."

"And how do we pay for them?" Ryan asked.

"We don't," Marty grinned, "we get the French to."

Marty contacted Wickham and asked him if he knew of any banks the French held significant funds in, within ten miles of the coast. Wickham showed up at the farm two days later.

"What are you up to Martin?" he asked, as he walked into Marty's office.

Marty looked at him in surprise and then twigged what triggered the question.

"We need funds," Marty replied.

"And you are planning to rob a French bank to get them?"

"Seemed like a working idea." Marty said sitting back in his chair.

"And what do you need these funds for?"

"To build specialist landing boats so we can get the Marines on shore fast and off again even faster." Marty explained what they had discussed and the conclusion they came to.

"And you can't use Navy boats to do this?" Wickham asked.

"We could use whaleboats, they are seaworthy enough and are pretty much the design we had in mind but as far as I know there aren't a lot of them laying around waiting to be requisitioned and, anyway, we want bigger versions than those available."

Wickham frowned as he thought it through.

"I don't want you tipping our hand so early in the war by robbing a bank," Wickham concluded.

"They would never know it was us," Marty reassured him.

"Maybe so." Wickham replied unconvinced. "However, I can provide funding for these boats. How many do you need and how much will they cost."

"I need to get up to fifty men ashore at a time so five boats plus a spare. We will 'acquire' another sloop sized ship like the Alouette or, preferably, an ex-whaler. That would carry most of the Marines and at least four of the boats. The other will go on the Alouette. I will get a price from the local shipwrights."

"And the Lark?"

"Too old now. She's passed her prime and we will just use her for cross channel work."

There was a knock on the door.

"Enter," Marty called.

James came in and looked quizzically at them both.

"James will command the second ship and Ryan Thompson will be on The Alouette with me." Marty stated.

Understanding dawned in James' eyes.

Wickham stood and said.

"I am going back to London after lunch. That du Demaine chap is still cooking here isn't he? I want to know how much the boats are going to cost me as soon as possible."

After one of Roland's excellent lunches, he put his coat on and picked up his hat.

"You will be paying me back for this," he said in parting.

"What did that mean?" James asked Marty after they heard the front door close.

"What the 'paying him back' comment?" Marty asked.

James nodded.

"He will either take the loan out of our next prize money or will want us to do a job off the record. That's my guess. Now get yourself down to the shipwrights and get me a price for our oversized whalers."

Marty took Thompson along as his clerk and met with La Pierre to inspect the Marines. He now had sixty of them plus two sergeants and Lieutenant La Pierre.

"We need to know what 'special' skills all these fine gentlemen have," he said. "Would you mind if I asked them a few questions?"

"Be my guest," La Pierre said intrigued.

"Gentlemen, as you know this is a special unit that does things the rest of the Navy doesn't. Now there are special skills we need so if any of you have experience in the following make yourselves known to Midshipman Thompson."

He looked at a piece of paper he had in his hand.

"Poacher." There was a laugh. He looked up when nobody moved and repeated. "Poacher." Three men stepped forward and went to Thompson who took their names.

"Pickpocket."

"Housebreaker."

"Cat burglar."

"What if I 'as more than one?" a particularly shifty man asked.

"Then you give your name each time." More laughs and comments as men were teased.

"Lockpick or smith."

"Forger."

"Roof man."

"Conman."

He continued listing every known felony. When he had finished there were just six men stood in the original ranks.

"And what do you good men do that can be of use to me?"

"I was training as a clock maker before I joined the Marines," one said.

"Blacksmith." said another.

"Always been a marine," said another who's face showed he enjoyed a fight.

"Farrier."

"What's the difference between that and a blacksmith?" asked Thompson

"A farrier looks after horses' feet and legs as well as makes shoes," the Marine told him. "Blacksmiths do general ironwork."

"Aye but some of us can do real fine stuff," the other marine boasted.

"What about you two?" Marty asked the last pair.

"I was a farm hand. Got a girl in to trouble and had to leave the village. I didn't want ter marry her, but her father had other ideas." Confessed one.

"I was a clerk, but I was bored so joined the Marines for some excitement."

Marty looked at the 'farm hand' and noted he had fine hands. He beckoned him to one side and said quietly.

"Those hands have never touched a plough or a pitchfork. What did you really do?"

The man looked embarrassed and said, "I was an artist. I joined the marines to get material for some action paintings and got trapped by it. I just love the excitement. These buggers would never let me hear the end of it if I admitted that," he confessed.

"Well you can make a real contribution if you can make maps and draw coastlines." Marty offered. "It's something the rest of them cannot do, and I'm sure you will only get some good-natured teasing to start with until they see the value."

"Aye sir, that I can," he agreed.

Marty went to La Pierre who was looking over the list.

"Well Paul what do we have then?" he asked.

The lieutenant gave him an amused look.

"What we have are the dregs of humanity. The rejects from every gaol from Ramsgate to Lincoln. I could start my own criminal empire."

Marty laughed

"This is Hood's idea of suitable material for the SOF, but it does give us an idea of how to structure our raids. Now there are these three," he indicated the blacksmith, farrier and clockmaker. "I have an idea we could use them to make special equipment for our missions. What do you think of the idea of setting them up in a workshop?"

"Hmm yes I can see that would be useful. Do you have something in mind to get them started?" Paul asked.

"When I was in Paris, I needed a timer to detonate an explosive charge, and I had an inkling that you might be able to use the works from a clock to do it. I would like to throw that at them for starters."

"That should challenge them. I will get them started," Paul replied thoughtfully.

James came back with an estimate of the costs to make the whalers from the shipwrights and Marty wrote that up in a letter and sent it by hand.

"Now all I need is to find a second ship." Marty thought

The Alouette sailed close to the wind south of Dunkirk. She flew the French flag and stayed clear of the British blockade. They had been told by their smuggler friends that the French whaling fleet, that was run by some fellow called Roch out of Dunkirk, had been seized by Napoleon. The ships were built on American lines, were very seaworthy and had davits for whale boats fitted on either side. They intended to acquire one of those ships to use in their depravations of the French coast.

To do that, they intended to sail into Dunkirk at dusk and moor close to the impounded ships. Then undercover of dark send a cutting crew across, take over the chosen vessel and sail it out. Simple.

The sailed into the funnel shaped inlet close on the heels of another French ship and could see the fort at the end clearly. A signal soared up above the ramparts, the daily recognition signal that was promptly answered by the other ship. James was watching for this and had the same signal bent on and travelling up the mast as fast as he could.

A guard boat rowed towards them with what could only be a pilot in the bow. Marty groaned this was not going to plan!

The Pilot boarded and Marty greeted him politely. He was directed to steer The Alouette down the channel towards the narrow end of the funnel.

"*Do we have to moor so far down?*" he asked.

"*For protection yes. The Roast Beefs have been known to, as they say, cut out ships that moor away from the protection of the guns.*"

"*But we are an armed privateer with a full crew. I think we will give the British bastards a bloody nose if they try that on us.*"

The pilot looked around at the crew. They had far more men than even a French country ship would carry, and they were notoriously overmanned.

"*Ha! Maybe you are right. There is a buoy over there. It is on the edge of the guns cover and I can get to my dinner all the faster,*" he laughed.

Marty swung them over to the buoy he had indicated. They were in luck so far as the ships they were targeting were all tied up next to each other a short way further in. They were most definitely under the protection of the guns.

Once the pilot had left Marty viewed the tied-up Whalers with a glass. Annoyed he slammed it shut.

"Problem skipper?" asked James.

"Not a stitch of canvas on the yards," he barked.

"We will have to tow her out?" Thompson chipped in from behind him.

"Dammit, but it certainly looks like it."

He took another look before the light completely failed.

"Looks like she is just tied to the next ship across. There are three together and then another three behind them. Get the cutting crew together and prepare the boats as soon as its fully dark. I want half the men back here once you secure the whaler to help with the sweeps. We are going to need them and the sails to get out of here."

Two hours later the boats left. Marty ordered The Alouette cast off and they gently started her towards the whaler under the sweeps. James set a shuttered lamp, that could only be seen from ahead, on the bow of the whaler as soon as they boarded to give Marty something to steer for.

Marty was concentrating on bringing The Alouette up to the right point to swing her around so they could attach a tow, when there was a barked query from just off the port beam.

"Hey there on the corvette, what are you doing?"

It was a guard boat. One of the men was stood holding a lantern and peering up at the side.

Marty walked over to the side trying to appear casual.

"Our mooring has slipped, damn my crew for a bunch of incompetent idiots, and we are now trying to find the buoy again," he shouted across. *"Do you know where there is one nearby?"*

"For a brandy we will show you!" laughed the guard.

"If you come aboard and help us, I will give you a bottle!"

The guards pulled up alongside and the crew help them tie up alongside. They came up the side grinning like cats who had got the canary. They were very quickly subdued by Tom and the Basques and tied up.

"When they wake up, they aren't half going to be embarrassed," Tom remarked with a grin, slapping his blackjack into his palm.

They made the turn and one of the boats came up pulling a messenger cable that they used to haul a hawse over the stern. The light blinked twice. They were free and ready to be towed. The returning crew swarmed up the side and the boat made fast.

Marty wet a finger and held it up. There was the faintest of breezes coming up from the south. They would have to do this just with the sweeps for the time being.

He warned the men against making unnecessary noise and they started to row. He had three men to a sweep, and they had to pull hard.

At first nothing seemed to be happening but then they started to move. Slowly so slowly they started to make headway. Marty checked his watch; they were still at slack tide. It would be another thirty minutes or more before the tide turned and started going out.

Time dragged and it seemed they were making such slow progress it would be light before they were out of the harbour.

He felt the ship move slightly differently. The tide had turned! It was easier but they were still changing the oarsmen every ten minutes, and the men were getting tired.

He was just beginning to think they would have to give up on the whole enterprise when he felt a slight increase in the breeze.

"Set the courses," he hissed.

The triangular sails filled then went slack.

"Damn!"

Then another puff of breeze and they filled again. He felt their pull immediately, but it still wasn't enough.

He ran to the stern and looked back at their charge. James was keeping her as straight as he could. The hawse was lifting out of the water as their speed picked up.

"Keep them rowing, two men to an oar," he commanded.

He walked down the line of sweating men. One looked to be struggling so he tapped him on the back and told him to move over as he took the oar himself.

Oar butt forward, dip and pull, raise the blade, oar butt forward and repeat.

He got into the rhythm and sweat ran down his face.

Then Tom was stood in front of him, hands on the oar stopping him. Marty looked at him, surprised.

"The sails have it now skipper," he said and looked up.

Marty followed his gaze and sure enough the sails were full and pulling. He looked across the moonlit bay and saw they were at the mouth of the harbour. They were clear! A cannon fired from the fort, but the ball fell far away from them. The French had woken up far too late.

"Get those men back in their boat and cast them adrift," he ordered pointing to the French guards.

Late morning found two ships sailing towards the English coast. One looked as if it was wearing a set of borrowed sails, as they didn't sit right on the yards, but she was moving under her own power and that was what counted. They were an odd pair. A Sloop of War and a Whaler who had the day's recognition signal, so were left to proceed unchallenged.

Back at the dock Marty and James set about inspecting their acquisition and were starting to be quite pleased. She couldn't be more than two or maybe three years old with sound timbers. Her bottom needed a clean and coppering due to being moored up for too long and her rigging needed tensioning, but she was sound and her three masts solid. There were no guns fitted and there was no canvas on board, but that could be remedied. She had davits for four boats which was perfect for what they wanted. She also had the big brick oven that was used to render down whale blubber to oil, which would be removed.

She needed a refit so Marty contacted Admiral Hood, reported that they had succeeded in finding their second ship and could he please buy her in so they could get her to Chatham. Hoods reply was by return and the Honfleur joined the Royal Navy. A month at the docks, and some spectacular bribes, saw her fitted out as an armed troop transport with new sails and a clean, newly coppered, bottom.

She only needed about thirty crew to sail her but the new whale boats needed eight men each to row them so she would carry a complement of sixty men and forty marines. Armament-wise they fitted her out with twelve-pound longs for artillery support of the shore party rather than for fighting a sea battle. All in all, she was about perfect, and a delivery of men recruited from the pubs in Maidstone by Ryan Thompson, and a purse full of shillings, meant they were ready to go.

Chapter 12: Bang on Time

Marty was in his study at the farm when there was a knock at the door.

"Enter" he called and in walked the three men he had tasked with making a timer.

"We has figured out how to make a timer for settin' off bombs sir," the watch smith, Private Harbrook, reported. Marty had almost forgotten about that with all the running around to get the Honfleur and fit her out.

"Excellent," he said.

"We would like to   " he looked to his colleague who muttered something "demonstriate it," he smiled at Marty, happy to get that out of the way.

"And how will you do that?" Marty asked.

Harbrook was nudged by Private Dibble, the blacksmith, who stepped forward and carefully placed a mechanism on the table in front of Marty.

Marty picked it up. It was made of brass and consisted of a clockwork mechanism housed in a cylinder with a graduated dial on the top. At the other end was, what looked like, a wheellock.

"You set the time you want the bomb to go off on the dial at the top." Explained Dibble. "Each notch is ten seconds." Marty looked at the dial and saw that there was a knob in the centre with an arrow engraved in it. "You turns that there knob to the number of 10 seconds you want. So, a minute be six notches."

Private Collins, the farrier, elbowed him in the ribs and whispered, "he do know that yer burk he be edewcated."

Dibble glared at him and continued. "When the timer has got all the way back here," he pointed to a graduation with a '0' engraved on it, "it sets off the wheel lock and the sparks fire the charge. Only don't knock it or it might trip the lock afore you are ready"

"May I?" Marty asked and all three nodded.

He set the timer for thirty seconds and set it on the table. The mechanism started to tick and dead on the count of thirty he was making in his head, the wheel lock spun sending out a shower of sparks.

"Boom," he said quietly.

He questioned the men about how they came up with the design and they told him how they had tried lots of different designs, but many had just been too fragile or too complicated. Then they had gone to London and talked to a clockmaker Harbrook knew, without telling him what it was for, and between them they had come up with a simple, but reliable, clockwork timer. Then they had to make it sturdy enough to take some knocks and figure out how to fire the powder. They had tried to fit a flintlock mechanism, and even made several, but they didn't work very well. Then they had the idea to use a wheel lock and figured out how to attach and trigger it.

"So how long do these take to make and how much do they cost?" Marty asked.

"That's the best bit," declared Dibble. "Now we has the design we can knock out three a week if we can get the brass. The materials cost five bob a time"

"More than enough," Marty said thoughtfully. "How many have we got already?"

"This one, and two others." Collins stated.

"Get another ten made," Marty ordered, "and get ready for a live demonstration."

"Wiv real powder?"

"With real powder. Well done all of you, there will be an extra guinea each for you next pay day."

A week later Admiral Hood and William Wickham were stood on a cold beach wondering what the hell Marty was doing. All he had told them was that he wanted to demonstrate an innovative new weapon to them and that had been enough to get them there.

"Gentlemen, in precisely two minutes and thirty seconds, this keg of powder will detonate," said Marty pointing at a small keg that was immediately in front of them. "You will notice there are no fuses running to it and no wires or other mechanisms to trip a lock." He picked the keg up carefully and showed them by holding it above his head. "Yet, it is primed and ready to explode exactly when we want it to." He put it down and took both men by the arm and moved them away. When they were at a safe distance, he took out his watch and said.

"One minute to go."

"How the hell?" started Hood and stopped as Marty held up his hand and said.

"Forty-five seconds."

Wickham looked intrigued.

"Thirty seconds."

Marty grinned at him and looked back to his watch.

"Fifteen, fourteen, thirteen, twelve, eleven, ten, nine, eight, seven, six, five, four, three, two,"

BOOM! The keg went up and bits of wood and sand flew skyward. Gulls shrieked and the men watching cheered.

"By God! How did you do that?" Hood spluttered amazed at the accuracy of the detonation.

"If you would like to come back to the farm all will be revealed." Marty said and nodded to Tom who got the men cleaning up the evidence.

Marty gave the boys the privilege of explaining their design to the two worthies. Once completed, and they had received praise for their ingenuity, he sat with Hood and Wickham in his study.

"A reliable timer for detonating bombs opens up a host of possibilities." Wickham observed. "However, I would not want it to be generally available."

"I agree," nodded Hood. "In the wrong hands this could cause chaos."

"We could offer you exclusivity." Marty grinned cheekily.

"Don't let your commercial successes go to your head youngster" Hood responded. "I believe this was invented by Navy personnel on Navy time so it's ours."

"We should reward the men somehow though," Marty pleaded.

"Very worthy of you to argue their cause my boy. What did you have in mind?"

"A shilling for every one they make was what I had in mind. It's not enough to turn their heads but will encourage them to come up with more ideas."

"I can live with that," Hood agreed, and Wickham nodded.

"Good. That's settled," Marty said and then looked at Wickham and asked.

"How many do you want?"

"Ten for now, delivered to my house discreetly. I will pay you the ten shillings on receipt."

"But…" Marty started to say something and then caught on. "Ah, it's payback time."

Wickham just smiled as he sat back in his chair with his hands folded over his stomach.

Chapter 13: Evolutions

The Honfleur was finally fully equipped with her boats and Marty decided to try out a practice landing or two. He selected Studland bay in Dorset for no other reason than it gave him the chance to visit his family and holdings down there. It did, coincidently and quite secondarily, resemble beaches along the coast of France and offer a certain amount of privacy.

The Alouette, now named The Swan while they were in British waters, and the Honfleur set sail on the early morning tide and headed down the coast. The weather cooperated for once and was fine with a steady West-south-westerly breeze. They arrived mid-afternoon and Marty had the two ships anchor a half mile off shore. He called the boat captains, Lieutenant La Pierre and his sergeants to a briefing.

"The idea here is to get fifty marines ashore in good order as close together as possible and at the same time. To do that the boats will need to form up in a line, far enough apart to not get their oars tangled and maintain that line to the beach.

Once ashore the marines are to skirmish into the dunes and then return to the boats to debark back to the ships. Any questions so far?"

Nobody stepped forward so he continued.

"This is your first try at this, so I don't expect it to be perfect. Boat captains step forward."

The men stepped forward and Marty got them into a line.

"Six boats. In this order. Make sure you remember who is either side of you. The approach will be led by the number three boat. That's you Ryan."

Midshipman Thompson nodded to acknowledge the honour. "To make this easy we will start with all boats in the water without their marines and just practice forming up in line. Once you have got that down, you will move on to rowing to shore in line. Once you have that, we will start practicing loading the boats with marines and taking them ashore."

Marty stood on the quarterdeck of the Alouette and watched the boats trying to sort themselves into order. It was quite frankly a shambles. He blew a whistle and ordered them back to their stations beside the ships. When they got back, he ran through the ideal routes for each boat in his mind based on their starting position. He went to the stern rail and shouted across to James.

"Re-number the boats as follows!" He then pointed to each boat in turn and renumbered them. Ryan Thompson's boat was still number three. But he re-numbered the shoreward boat at the bow of the Honfleur as **two**, the seaward side **one**, the one nearest the shore at the stern **four** and the one on the seaward side **five**.

"Try again," he shouted and signalled the depart.

This time it went much better as the boats didn't have to cross each other. They did it another four times and it worked well.

"Ok this time when you are in line, make for the beach," he called.

They got into position just fine but as they made towards the beach, they had a tendency to bunch up and clash oars. That resulted in a lot of shouting and cursing as they blamed each other for not staying straight.

He got them all back on board and asked what the problem was. It turned out that as they were all in a line, they had no reference point to steer by and they tended to drift one way or the other. They talked about possible solutions when one of the mates suggested in a broad Yorkshire accent.

"If we were all a bit behind each other like geese do fly, then we would 'av some points we could line up on t'other boat and keep us place like."

Marty laughed; it was so obvious when pointed out. He put his hand in his pocket, pulled out a guinea and flipped it to the sailor.

"Norris isn't it? he said. "Where did you get that idea?"

"I were a wildfowler back in the day and I would watch the geese fer ages and never saw one run 'is beak up another one's arse." he replied causing the room to dissolve into laughter.

After the men had their lunch, they tried it again. The echelon formation worked a treat. The boats went in in an arrowhead and all hit the beach within a minute of each other. Getting off was simple, the men just turned around and faced the other way while the boat captain shipped the rudder to the shore end then they just rowed out.

Satisfied that all was well, and all the men and boats were safely back aboard, Marty ordered his gig brought around and manned. He jumped in last and saw that it was manned by Tom, John and the Basques. With a grin he ordered them to sail around the headland into Poole harbour then up the Frome to Wareham. They moored up at the wharf and Marty told the boys to make themselves comfortable at the Shovel and Crown pub. He would make his way to his mother's house.

Tom was having none of that. He would go with him as escort.

"Lady Caroline would have my hide if'n anything happened to you," was his excuse.

Marty rented a carriage from the Red Lion and the two of them went across the causeway to Stoborough and on to Furzebrook. It was just getting dark as they pulled up at the house. Marty paid the coachman and asked to be picked up at dawn.

He could see a face at the window so called out.

"It's me Mum. Marty!"

The door opened and his brother Alf was there grinning.

"Don't you ever give any warning when you be visiting?" He joked grabbing Marty in a hug.

"Wotcher Tom," he said shaking the big man's hand. "Aint seen you since the wedding."

"Is Mum inside?" Marty asked.

"Yeah. She is." Alf replied. "We've tried to get her to move over to Church Knowle with the rest of us, but she says she will stay here. 'Her Marty got her this place, and this is where she will die,' she says. Tis my turn to stay with her this week. We don't like to leave her on her own and she won't 'ave anyone but family here with her."

Marty squared his shoulders and went into the house. His mother and grandfather, who was still hanging on at a grand old age, were sat in the parlour. His mother's eyes filled up when she saw him, and he bent to hug her. She kissed him on the cheeks.

'Look at you!" she said looking him over. He was in his second-best lieutenant's uniform with his hanger and knife on his belt.

He pulled up kitchen chairs for him and Tom leaving Alf the third comfortable chair.

"It's been a long time since you visited last," she cajoled him, "but you be here now, and you did write."

Marty laughed and said. "It's a bit difficult to pop home from India mum."

"Did it really take five month to get there?" asked Alf who had only been as far as London for their wedding, and that had taken ages even with Marty paying for coaches for all of them.

"It certainly did, and three months to get back," Marty replied. "I brought you this Mum." He said taking a package wrapped in brown paper from Tom and handing it to her. She opened it and inside was a beautiful Indian silk shawl. It was a vibrant blue and had a deep burgundy fringe around the edge.

"Oh my, that be beautiful," she exclaimed and wrapped it around her shoulders.

"I also have to tell you that Caroline will be bringing the babes down to visit. Mountjoy will be with her so he can do a proper plan and inventory of the estate and they will be staying for a couple of months. She wants the kids to know who their family is."

"That will be just grand!" Annie said and got a dreamy look in her eye at the thought of more kids running around.

They talked until Annie got tired and then went to bed. The coach was waiting for them at dawn.

Back on The Alouette, they began then next evolution which was getting the Marines on to the boats. They thought of slinging cargo nets over the side but that proved awkward and the marines solved the problem themselves by just shinnying down the drop ropes from the davits to get down into the boats. On The Alouette they used the entry port. They would sling nets for them to re-board.

The marines were treating the whole thing as a competition and Marty was fairly sure bets were being placed on which boats would be loaded quickest.

'All incentives to get this working efficiently,' he told himself, *'but I must have a word with them about the noise.'*

The boats were loaded, and they set off towards the beach. The echelon formation worked well. The boats ran up on the sand and the marines jumped over the side at the bow to avoid getting their feet wet. La Pierre had them formed up on the beach in short order and skirmishers (the poachers and a couple of footpads) were already heading inland. Marty spotted a familiar brindled shape running beside them.

'How the hell did he get ashore?'

Marty called up his gig and joined them on the beach.

"Paul, can you get the men gathered around please," he asked and went to stand on a small dune where everyone could hear him.

"First of all, well done everyone. You managed that without dropping anyone or your kit over the side and did it in a good time. I think there was some competition going on and I would like to officially state that the number four boat loaded fastest." Cheers and groans from the gathered marines as some made money and others lost.

"But as you all loaded in a good time there will be an extra rum ration for all of you." Cheers all around at that.

"Now in future when we do this off the enemy coast, noise will be the enemy. You will have to do this silently."

There was a ripple of laughter from the back of the crowd that moved forward towards him. He paused, puzzled as to what was causing it and watched as Blaez emerged from the crowd with a fat rabbit in his mouth. He walked up to Marty, dropped the rabbit at his feet then sat looking expectantly at him.

"Joined the poachers have you boy," he said as he ruffled his head.

"Would appreciate it if he didn't accompany you when you do this for real unless I am with you," he told the assembled men with a smile.

"We will return to the ships. I want you all back on board as fast as possible. We might need to get away quickly in future so let's practice that now."

They spent the rest of the day practicing beach landings and Marty decided that another day of practice wouldn't hurt so they overnighted again in the bay. They were starting the last practice in the afternoon when he saw a small group of people stood on the dunes. He got a telescope and took a closer look.

It was Caroline, his children, Mountjoy, mother and his brother Alf. Caroline waved as she saw he was looking at them. He waved back and called for his gig.

On shore he walked up the dunes, greeted Caroline with a huge hug and kiss and picked up Bethany and James in turn and kissed them. He hugged his mother and shook hands with Mountjoy and Alf.

"Be both of those boats yourn?" his mother asked.

"They are ships mum, and yes they are," he relied with a smile of pride.

"And all them men runnin' around on the beach?"

"Yes those too."

"What they doin' thet fer?"

"They are practicing invading France," he exaggerated getting a kick in the ankle from Caroline.

"Well they be a fierce looking bunch o' ner-do-wells. That Napoleon don't stand much of a chance do 'e," she said seriously.

Marty hid a smile. At that moment he loved his mother more than he ever had.

"Did you just arrive?" he asked Caroline.

"We got to your mother's house just before noon. We had lunch and then Alf mentioned you were in the bay and said it was only an hour or so by coach," she replied

"He never did have much of a head for distance. It's more like two hours." Marty laughed. "Are you all going back to the cottage or straight to Church Knowle?"

"We are ALL going back to Church Knowle." Caroline said with a sly look at Alf. "He bet me that I couldn't get your mother to stay there."

"She cheated," Alf chipped in. "She got Beth to do the asking and there aint a force on earth that can refuse that babe when she uses them eyes."

Marty laughed, he had plenty of experience of his precocious daughter using her whiles to get her own way. His mother never stood a chance.

He was suddenly aware that the marines were manoeuvring in skirmish line right for them. His mother's eyes went wide, and he quickly reassured her that she was quite safe. The forward scouts passed by rapidly with an "afternoon all" and a salute. Then positioned themselves on the back face of a dune twenty yards inland. The rest of the marines moved up to the ridge Marty and his family were stood on and formed two ranks. The front rank knelt and, to the shouted orders of La Pierre, raised their muskets and fired a volley. The second rank took a step forward to the front and then they knelt and loosed off a volley as well.

To finish it off the ships fired a timed fourteen-gun salute. Annie was flushed with excitement and James and Alf were whooping at every bang. Beth was in her mother's arms not sure if she liked it or not, Caroline was grinning. Marty laughed, as there was no such thing as a fourteen-gun salute in the Navy, so this was just for them.

Back on board, with his family safely on their way to the manor house at Church Knowle, Marty had called his officers into his quarters. They were all grinning happily, and he thanked them for their unexpected initiative. He then dismissed them with orders to get underway and set course for their home base.

He had dinner with Paul La Pierre, and they were tucking into the rabbit Blaez had caught when la Pierre suddenly said.

"You must be the luckiest man alive Martin."

"Why's that?" Marty asked.

"You have one of the most beautiful women in England for your wife, two lovely children, you have more money than the King, and you get to play with ships almost on your own terms. The only question is why do you keep doing this?" he asked gesturing at the ship around them.

"That's easy to answer," he said. "It's so I can keep what I have, have the freedom to enjoy it and have my children live in a free country so they can enjoy it after me."

Chapter 14: A Fiery Baptism

Marty ran his finger down the French coastline. It was time for their first operation in anger and he wanted a target that was worthwhile but not too challenging.

Napoleon was building up his forces for what looked like an invasion of Britain and he wanted to avoid places where there were concentrations of troops. Calais, Dunkirk, Boulogne were counted out. Brest was being blockaded so that was out too. He also didn't want to hit ports that were used by the smugglers. That would be like cutting holes in his own pocket. He needed more information.

He went down to Deal and found Bill Clarence, the head of the smugglers that they worked with. He was in the Waggon and Horses chatting with the landlord, Frank, whose daughter Susie had married Armand a couple of years before.

"Bill, Frank, are you well?" Marty greeted them.

"Marty! Nice to see you again! You bin a right stranger," Frank exclaimed.

"He bin in fields afar," Bill grinned pumping his hand. "Look at his colour, he be as dark as one of them Indian fellers."

"That's 'cus I was there for close on the last three years," Marty replied extracting his hand before it was crushed. "I was sorry to miss the wedding Frank."

"Ay it were a bit of a do," Frank smiled wistfully "She looked beautiful she did."

"Where is Armand now then?" Marty asked.

"Over in Calais at the moment," Bill replied. "Keepin' an eye on the build-up of troops and the like. Took 'im o'er meself about a fortnight ago."

Just them Susie came out of the backroom and seeing Marty screamed and rushed over to him. He got stood up just in time to catch her as she threw herself into his arms.

"Look at you!" she said pushing him away so she could look at him. "Armand said you be commin' back. "Is Caroline with you?"

"She's in Dorset with my family," Marty told her. "She wants the kids to know where their dad comes from."

"And so they should. I just wish we could take young Jessica over to meet his people," Susie sighed.

"Is she around? I'd love to meet her," Marty said.

"She be 'aving a nap now, but if you are still here in an hour she will be awake then," Susie replied then said, "Well I can't stand here yacking all day, I got to get them pies baked."

"See you later then," Marty said and patted her behind as she turned away. She flicked him a glance over her shoulder as she walked away and stuck out her tongue.

"Now," Marty said as he sat back down. "When can you get me over to Calais?"

The docks at Calais were largely deserted when Marty jumped ashore from the fishing boat that had brought him from Deal. The British blockade was heavily restricting trade, but the fishing fleet was being left largely unmolested. The smugglers were welcome as they were one of the only reliable sources of income for many people.

He made his way to an address Bill had given him on the Eastern edge of town. It was a house owned by a sympathiser where Armand was supposed to be based. He knocked on the door and an elderly man answered.

"Hello. Can I interest you in some fine woollen cloth?" Marty asked.

"Why yes! The season is changing, and snow is on its way," the man responded and invited him in.

He led Marty through to an upstairs room at the back of the house which had a spectacular view out over the area that the French army were staging their troops. Armand was sat in a comfortable chair with a large telescope on a tripod in front of him, watching the troops movements and making notes.

He looked up and saw who had come to visit.

"*Martin!*" he yelped and stood up to hug him and kiss his cheeks. *"What are you doing here?"*

The old man muttered something about coffee and left.

"*Why I just had to visit my old friend now he is an old married man,"* he joked. *"You are looking very well on it."*

"*Pphhtt, that is Susie's cooking. She makes the most wonderful pies,"* he boasted.

They sat and chatted while the old man came in with a tray of coffee and pastries. Once he had left Marty told Armand about their new brief and capability.

"*Tshh, those two always want more,"* he said referring to Hood and Wickham.

"*What do you need from me?"*

"*Information. I need to know where we can have a real impact,"* Marty told him.

"*Hmm well let me think. You can discount Calais and Dunkirk. There is an infantry brigade stationed near Gravelines and they have a large ammunition store away from their camp. If you blew that up, they would hear it in London."*

"*Maybe later when we have had some practice."* Marty smiled.

"*There is a boatyard at Le Touquet that is building barges for transporting soldiers. Burning that would be good."* Armand said thoughtfully. *"There is an army contingent down there and an office of the ministry of marine, and where there is an office"*

"*There is gold for payment,."* they finished together laughing.

Marty briefed his team carefully. He did it in a totally different way than any other commander in the Navy. He had managed to get a map of the town of Le Touquet and the surrounding lands and had got John and the artistic marine to make a large-scale version, which he had pinned up on the wall. He had not only the officers but non-coms down to corporal in the briefing.

"We have two targets for our raid on Le Touquet," he began. "The first is the shipyards where they are building barges for Napoleon's invasion fleet. They need to be burnt to the ground. The second target is the Ministry of Marine building here in the town." He pointed to the locations with a long stick. "Lieutenant La Pierre will brief you on the teams and plan."

"I will lead the shipyards team with Sergeant Edney. The team will be made up thirty men in five, six-man squads each led by a corporal. These men will deploy from the drop off point here on the beach and proceed north to the estuary where the boatyards are located here." He indicated an area just inside the estuary on its south bank. "Four squads will burn the yards and the other two will cover these two access roads and make sure we are not disturbed. That will be Corpr'l Stokes team here and Corpr'l Everett's here.

The second team will deploy from the same drop off point and will be led by Lieutenant Stockley and Sergeant Bright. This team will be twenty men in two squads of ten. The forward scouts, the house breakers and cat burglars will be in this team," he added with a grin.

"Not to mention the lock picks and pick pockets," Marty added as he stood to take over.

"The teams will be led by myself and the good Sergeant. Mine will be responsible for entering and searching the Ministry building. Sergeant Bright will secure the area and our line of escape. There is a contingent of French Infantry in the area so if the alarm goes up, we may have to fight our way out of town. Any questions?"

They carried on for another half hour about timings and the signals, which would be given by rockets as the whole attack would be done by the full moon. If all went well the whole thing would be over in a couple of hours.

It was beautiful clear night as the two ships ghosted along under minimum sail. The Milky Way was clearly visible as a huge smear of stars across the heavens and the occasional shooting star was seen to cleave Orion's Belt.

As they saw the outlines of the landmarks that surrounded Le Touquet come into line Marty knew they had reached the correct position and ordered the foresails backed. The backward pressure of the foresails was balanced by the thrust of the main and mizzen topsails and the ship came to a silent halt.

The whalers were lowered to the water and the crews shinnied down the ropes to take their positions at the oars. Once they were set the marines came down the ropes and silently took position along the centreline. The shipyard team carried un-primed, but loaded muskets, a fearsome selection of edged weapons and the necessary materials to set the boatyards ablaze. Martin's raiding party carried the same array of weaponry but had bread sacks tucked through their belts to carry documents back with them.

Marty waited until he got the signal from the Honfleur that they were ready and jumped down into his boat. He looked at his men. They all had dark clothes and blackened faces. The purser had bought in a stock of cork just for this purpose. Burnt cork mixed with a bit of fat made a superb face black.

The boats formed up on Marty's, which was number three and would be the point of the echelon with Ryan Thompson commanding it. When they were set, he gave the command to row for the beach. They went at a steady pace and the oars were muffled with cloths around the oarlocks to minimize noise.

The boat glided up on to the sand and the marines made their way forward to jump over either side of the bow while a couple of sailors jumped over either side and steadied the boat, stopping it turning.

The corporals got their squads together and the sergeants organised the corporals. Lieutenant La Pierre organised the Sergeants and the fire team moved out to the North. Sergeant Bright didn't give Marty a chance to interfere with his marines and got their two squads into shape and moving leaving Marty to run and catch up.

Marty thought he had left Blaez onboard, but a dark shape ran up beside him and settled down to pace him. *How the hell?* He thought but then the dog brushed against him and he suddenly had a very wet patch on his leg. *He swam ashore!* He realised. He was suddenly very proud of his companion.

The fire team made their way steadily along the beach. It was harder going than running on hard ground, so they stayed close to the waterline where the sand was firmer. As they got closer to the boatyards, they picked up the smell of freshly sawn wood and tar. The scouts, who ranged ahead suddenly stopped and a hand was held up. The marines immediately stopped and dropped to a knee. La Pierre and Sergeant Edney crept forward and dropped down beside them.

One of the scouts, private Sheldon, pointed to a glow coming from the first yard. La Pierre signed for him to go take a look by pointing to his eyes then the glow. Sheldon moved forward in a crouch silently testing the ground with every step. He got himself in a position where he could ease himself up the rickety fence and peek over the top. He dropped down immediately and worked his way back.

"Night watchman," he reported. "Old feller and another in the last yard. I kin see the glow of his fire."

"Awake?" asked La Pierre.

"Yes, sitting looking in ter the flames."

Perfect, he would be completely night blind.

"Take him out quietly. Don't kill him unless you have to."

"Aye aye sir!"

Sheldon slipped away, moving inland to get around the fence. He disappeared and all they could do was wait. La Pierre looked at his pocket watch. He could see it quite clearly by the full moon. They had been ashore for just fifteen minutes, but it felt much longer.

Sheldon reappeared and waved. They signalled the team and started moving forward again. He was waiting for them at the entrance to the yard.

"There be four or five men asleep in that hut over there. They looks like workers," he told La Pierre.

Paul thought for a minute and then ordered.

"Sergeant take the second security section and check the rest of the yards for residents then set up as planned on the far road. Report back here yourself."

"Where is Corporal Stringer?"

"Here sir!" a voice hissed from the side.

"Take your team and neutralise the inhabitants of that hut. Use blackjacks rather than knives. Get them out of the way and secure then get back to your positions as planned. Understood?"

"Aye aye sir."

Stringer's squad moved out, silent and efficient.

Blaez trotted along beside his boss. He had sensed that Marty was moving into danger and there was no way he was being left behind. Now he moved beside him with all his senses at heightened alert. The swim to shore, albeit over half a mile, hadn't been a problem, his paws were half webbed, and he swam like an otter. Now he was looking out for the things his boss couldn't see with his inferior senses.

Marty's team moved through the town like shadows. They were chosen for their special skills at moving silently and getting into places that would normally be secure. They were in a word, effective. The two point-men were woodsmen and could move silently through dry brush. They made no sound as they moved through the town. When they came upon a night watchman walking his rounds, he didn't know what hit him.

The ministry building was next door to l'Hotel de Ville, the town hall, and was perhaps a little ostentatious for post-revolutionary France. It was dark and there seemed to be no one on guard. They started to move in when Blaez growled low in his throat.

Marty immediately stopped and everyone else stopped at the same time. Sergeant Bright had heard the growl, pointed to two men and signalled for them to patrol to either side of the building.

There was the sound of a brief scuffle, no more than a second or two, then the marine who had gone around the left side of the building re-appeared and gave a thumbs up.

Marty waited for another minute until the second scout reappeared having gone completely around the building. When he gave a thumbs up, Marty moved up to the door, he was after all the best lock pick of the team.

The door took nine seconds to unlock and Marty quietly opened it with a blackjack in his left hand. He waited and listened, there was no sound from inside. He went to enter then froze. He had heard something but wasn't sure what it was. There! He heard it again. A snore!

Silently he slipped into the building. He didn't need to look behind him to know that his men would be following as they had practiced. Blaez pushed ahead, went straight to a door to the right and stood head cocked to one side listening.

Marty signalled for his men to move ahead and clear the rooms around the entrance hall. He moved over beside Blaez and slowly opened the door. Inside he could just make out the outline of a guard. He was laid out on a couch, fast asleep and snoring stentoriously. Marty moved over beside him and pinched his nose. He didn't wake but rolled onto his side. With a grin Marty rapped him sharply behind the ear with the blackjack then bound and gagged him.

Around about the same time as Marty put the guard into a deep sleep. La Pierre was looking at the result of his men 'cleaning up' the boatyards. There were seventeen, neatly trussed and gagged, men laid out along the side of the road. According to his watch they were about on schedule and Marty should be inside the ministry around now.

The search of the ministry was moving along well. They had collected several bagsful of papers, memos, and communiques. But so far, no gold. Marty chewed a nail. There had to be some here somewhere, but where?

La Pierre looked at his watch for the fourth or fifth time in as many minutes. It was time. "Sergeant signal for the fires to be set if you would be so kind," he asked.

Sergeant Edney reached into a pack and took out a small signal rocket. He took a burning piece of slow match from a marine and lit the fuse. He held the rocket at arm's length between two fingers and as soon as it whooshed into life he let it fly up into the pristine sky. The rocket painted a trail of blue light that sparkled as it fell earthward and faded.

Small fires blossomed and then grew into brilliant red and yellow flowers as they took hold of the seasoned wood. Soon the flames had grown into raging infernos that would rival a volcano for ferocity.

Back at the Ministry Marty stood in the main office and looked around. Nothing looked out of place. Then he heard scratching. He looked around and Blaez was pawing at a piece of carpet. He stopped and sniffed at it, cocked his head to one side and then pounced on it with both feet.

"What's that boy?" Marty asked. Blaez looked at him with the goofy look he had when he was ratting in the barn and he wanted Marty to move something so he could get to his prey.

Marty pulled the carpet aside and tapped with his foot on the floor, it was hollow. Marty looked carefully and saw a small hole, he put his finger in and felt around. He couldn't feel anything like a lock mechanism, so he hooked it and pulled.

Back at The Alouette, Marty watched the flames as both the boatyards and the ministry burnt merrily. He grinned and ordered Midshipman Thompson to make way and head back towards home. Returning to his cabin he looked at the small chest that was sat on his desk. It was heavy, that was not in doubt as he had carried it halfway back to the beach before one of the larger Marines had taken it from him with a grin and a "let me 'elp you there Sor."

He examined the lock, then opened a drawer on his desk and took out a small set of lock picks. He was just slipping them in when there was a knock at the door and Tom walked in.

"So that's the chest everyone is talking about," he said as he dropped into one of the chairs. "Where did you find it?"

"I didn't, he did." Marty answered nodding at Blaez who was demolishing a beef bone that the cook had given him. "There was rat in the hidden compartment under the floor and he heard it."

There was a click as the lock succumbed to his attentions and he popped open the clasp. He grinned at Tom and opened the lid. He frowned as he pulled out a packet of papers and then his eyebrows went up as he read them.

"These are the orders for the barges from the ministry in Paris and they aren't just for the boatyards that we burnt. They list what they want built from every boatyard along this stretch of coast. That office is, or rather was until we burnt it, the main controlling office for that whole sector."

"That's good, we will know where to go next, but what's in the rest of the box?" Tom asked obviously itching with curiosity.

"Oh, you mean this?" Marty said absently flipping him a coin.

"Lous d'Or. Nice! How many?"

"I don't know, why don't you count them." Marty said still distracted by the papers.

Tom looked at him and shook his head. Marty knew he couldn't count much above ten so he stood and opened the door.

"Marine Sheldon!" he bellowed

Marine Sheldon arrived in a hurry.

"Sah!" he shouted as he stamped to attention in front of Tom.

"You don't call me sir you idiot" Tom snapped, "and don't shout. I want you to count the coins in that chest."

Sheldon's eyes went wide, and his fingers twitched.

"And if you have any ideas about slipping one or two in your pocket I will be watching."

The count showed they had five hundred and eighty-three Louis, that was around one thousand, seven hundred and fifty pounds. A decent haul! Marty decided that half would go to Wickham to pay off their debt. The rest would be added to the men's social fund, which he had set up to ensure they would get an income if they were invalided out of the service, or their families would get something to live on if they were killed.

Marty sat in his office and marked all the boatyards that were listed in the papers on a map. St Valery, Cayeux, Ault,

Mers-le-Bains and Dieppe were the main ones with the biggest orders. He knew one thing for certain, someone would look for the chest in the burnt-out ruin of the ministry and realise it was missing. They would soon know they were coming. They needed to act fast before the French could react.

They had the ships ready for a second sortie two nights later and set sail at dusk. Their target was Mers-le-Bains. Dieppe was bigger but was also a Naval base for the French and he didn't want to walk into a hornet's nest without scouting it first. The plan was different this time. The marines would land on the beach as before, but then the Alouette would move up the coast a short way and bombard an army encampment between Ault and Friaucourt mentioned in the paperwork they had found.

The drop off went exactly to plan and they moved up the coast. Marty identified the town of Ault and the lookout on the mast reported seeing camp fires about a mile behind it. They would be shooting blind, but the sea was relatively flat, and they knew roughly how far inland the shot had to travel. Marty planned to 'walk' the barrage through the encampment by starting short and increasing the range by increments. Their long nines would just about have the range.

The hove to and the gunners set the quoins to the angle Marty had calculated. That in itself was an approximation as there were no graduations on a naval gun. They let fly the first broadside.

The lookout couldn't see the fall of shot so they raised the barrels a fraction and fired again. Still nothing although he did say that he could see torches moving around in the camp.

Up again and let fly. This time he reported that a couple of the campfires had thrown up sparks into the air. Marty let the next broadside go without changing anything. The lookout reported there were some new fires.

Marty grabbed a night glass and climbed the mainmast. Up and around the futtock shrouds to the topsail yard. He settled himself and moved the glass up from the town near them until he picked up the fires. Everything was upside down and back to front, but he could see men running around and a couple of burning tents.

The next broadside fired, and he waited.

The ground inside the camp erupted in geysers of dirt as the shot landed. Some must have ricocheted as there were tents being knocked down further back and a group of soldiers were bowled over like skittles. He shinned down a stay to the deck and ordered two more broadsides for effect and then they would return to Mers-le-Bains.

Chapter 15: Lost and Found

Back at base Marty had a conference with his mids, La Pierre, Simmonds, the Sailing Master, and Bill Clarence.

"What do we know about Dieppe?"

"It's an active port with two basins accessed through a channel from the sea. The inner basin is larger and is effectively a holding basin. The outer is where ships drop off and load goods." Simmonds informed them.

"The French have installed artillery to defend the entrance. You don't get in or out without permission," Bill added. "The last time we were there we saw a couple of frigates and a liner in the holding basin."

"Where are the boatyards?" Marty asked.

"At the back end of the holding basin. There are slips for building ships as well, they can build anything up to a corvette there." Bill answered.

"So how could we disrupt the port?" Marty asked realising an attack on the yards was out of the question.

"Well if you could sink a reasonable sized ship in the entrance channel you would close it until they could clear the wreck," Ryan Thompson suggested.

"They would just blow it up." Marty replied.

They were silent for a few minutes. Then James Campbell said thoughtfully.

"What if it was full of stone?"

"What if what was full of stone?" Marty asked him.

"The ship we sink in the harbour entrance. What if it was full of stone?" he replied.

"That isn't a bad idea!" Simmonds stated. "especially if it were full of big lumps of stone."

"What kind of ship?" James asked.

"Not a ship." Bill said. "A barge. Or even better two."

The discussion continued over dinner and focused on barges in particular. Barges were horrible sailors, they had flat bottoms and needed leeboards to stop them sliding sideways with the wind. A barge loaded with stone would be difficult to steer and be very low in the water so could only be sailed in very slight seas. Marty had seen some big barges working out of the Isle of Purbeck moving stone from there around the coast to London.

He wrote up their plan and sent it to Hood and Wickham. He wasn't surprised when he was summoned to a meeting at Wickham's house at short notice.

He rode up to Canterbury and then got a coach to London. He planned to stay over at his London house as Caroline and the children were still in Dorset but went straight to Wickham's house to be there on time.

After the usual pleasantries they waited for Lord Hood to arrive then got down to business.

"Do you think that sinking these barges will close the port for any length of time?" asked Hood. "I don't want us to waste a lot of effort and have them clear it in a couple of days."

"We plan to fill the holds with mortar to make it into one solid mass. It will act like a dam." Marty replied. "They will have to chip it out or blow it up bit by bit."

"Why two barges?" asked Wickham.

"The channel is narrow and relatively shallow," he explained, "so we plan to drop one along the channel and the other across it but just behind the first one." Marty drew a diagram on a sheet of paper as he explained. "That should seal it up for a long time."

"Where do you propose getting the barges and stone?" Hood asked even though it had told them in the letter.

"The barges they use for moving the stone from Purbeck or Portland up the coast to London would be perfect. They have a very high freeboard so they can carry heavy loads.

When loaded they are stable, they have a single mast, leeboards and are gaff rigged. They look a lot like a French stone barge as I guess there is only one design that works. The stone can be the rejected stuff that comes out of the mines. It's worth nothing so we can get it for the cost of loading it."

Hood sat back in thought. As he watched him Marty noticed how he was looking his 79 years of age. *He's done bloody well considering he was at sea for fifty-three years,* Marty thought as he waited for his judgement.

"It might just work," said Hood. "It would free up the channel fleet from blockading it, allowing them to focus on Brest. I think you should give it a go. I will talk to Troubridge and get him to endorse it."

Sir Thomas Troubridge was the First Navy Lord and his name on this would make it an official Navy mission. Marty would fail at his peril.

Marty returned to his house and sent an invitation to the de Marches family to come and visit that afternoon or on the morrow. Marty guessed he had at least that long to relax. His letter writing was up to date, so he decided to take a stroll. Blaez needed a walk and the weather was fine. He put his pocket pistols in his coat pocket, put on his bicorn hat and left.

Hyde Park was just at the end of Upper Grosvenor Street where they had their house, so it took only a few minutes for him to pass through the gate into the park proper. There were a lot of people making the most of the good weather and as he walked, he observed young couples walking side by side followed by a servant or older relative as chaperone. There were others, who were obviously married, walking or riding in open carriages with their children. There were even couples who were behaving in such a way as they could only be having a triste.

As he walked, he noticed a handsome couple, a Navy captain and a very beautiful woman walking arm in arm towards him. The man looked at him and grinned in recognition.

"Martin! How are you my boy?" cried Captain Turner in greeting and reached out to shake his hand.

Marty took it and shook it vigorously.

"I am extremely well Sir," he replied. "I had no idea you were ashore still."

"Will be joining my new ship on Monday, they've given me the Triton, a seventy-four." He got a nudge in the ribs from his companion. He started and then said, "allow me to introduce my fiancé, Juliette Harmason."

Marty made a leg over her proffered hand.

"Juliette, this is Lieutenant Martin Stockley otherwise known as Lord Candor," he finished with a grin.

"Ah the infamous Martee." Juliette smiled with wicked glint in her eye. "I heard about your early exploits from Contessa Evelyn. How is Lady Caroline?"

"She and the children are well and visiting my family in Dorset," Marty replied wondering if he would ever live Toulon down.

"Dorset?" asked Turner wondering where they would be staying given the status of Martin's family.

Marty saw the look on his face and guessed what he was thinking.

"We have acquired land and a manor house at Church Knowle. My family run the farm for us," he explained.

"Aah that makes sense of something my sister mentioned in a letter. You still write to her I hear."

Blaez chose that moment to get bored and he stood on his hind legs with his front paws on Marty's chest.

"Can we walk? Blaez has a short attention span," Marty laughed.

"He has quite a reputation, one to match yours," Turner stated.

Marty ruffled Blaez's ears and grinned, then turned to Juliette and teased, "so, you have managed to tame the good Captain! His sister and I were beginning to despair he would ever find the right woman, despite all his looking."

That started an exchange of stories that had Juliette in fits of giggles.

They had walked and talked for half an hour or so when Blaez suddenly pulled towards some bushes on the side of the road.

"What is it boy?" Marty asked. He let him pull him forward while he pulled a pistol from his pocket. The dog pushed into the bushes and then stopped and whined.

Marty pushed in as well and shouted.

"Captain! There is a girl in here! She's been attacked and hurt!"

"Juliette find a constable," Turner said, "I will help Martin."

She nodded and walked quickly back down the path to where they had seen a constable earlier.

Marty and Turner, meanwhile, gently extracted the young girl from the bushes, and made her comfortable covering her with Marty's coat. They could see she was probably from a middle-class family and about sixteen years old. Turner knelt by her and was checking her over for injuries when Juliette returned with a constable and another man that identified himself as a doctor.

"Any idea who she is Sir?" the constable asked Marty.

"Never seen her before. The dog found her in the bushes." Marty replied.

The constable looked at Blaez who gave him one of his direct looks back. He walked into the bushes and could be heard moving around. When he returned he held a purse.

"This was further back in there," he said and opened it. After a short rummage around he pulled out a visiting card. "Harold Mullins, Solicitor. Has a place in Chapel Street."

Marty looked at it and memorised the address.

"I will go and see him. He should know who she is." Marty told him. "The doctor has said he will take the girl to his practice. I will pay for any treatment she needs."

The constable took note of everyone's names and addresses and his eyebrows shot up when he found out who Marty was. He didn't object to Marty getting involved. He was, after all, just a Bow Street Runner.

Marty got a cab to the address on the card. It was in a middle-class area of London in the Lincolns Inn district. He walked up to the house and confirmed it was the right house by the name on the brass plaque by the door. He knocked.

A servant woman opened the door and Marty asked to see Mr Mullins and gave her his card. She let him into the hallway after giving Blaez a dirty look then disappeared to the back of the house. He heard a voice raised in question and then a portly man in a grey suit bustled out from the direction she had gone.

"My Lord Candor, what can I do for you? Please! Come in, come in," he insisted and took Marty into an office.

Marty told him about the girl he had found, and the colour drained from his face.

"You know the girl?" Marty asked.

"It must be my daughter, Annabelle," the man cried starting to stand. "Where is she?"

Marty told him about the doctor and offered to take him to her. The man, obviously in shock, just nodded so Marty took a coat from a stand inside the door and handed it to him as he led him outside. The same cab was waiting just down the street and Marty whistled to get his attention.

"Thought you wouldn't be long," said the driver, "so, I hung around like."

Once they were in and moving Marty asked, "do you have any idea who would do this?"

Mullins looked undecided whether to say something or not.

"I can't help you, if you don't tell me," Marty pressed.

Mullins looked at him and took hope from the steady brown eyes that looked back at him.

"I borrowed money from a money lender in Bethnal Green and I got behind on the payments even though I paid the capital back with interest. He has been increasing the amount of interest every week I am late, and I could never clear the debt now. He warned me that he would take it out on my daughter if I didn't pay up."

"Did he indeed," Marty muttered.

"He has a gang of enforcers, nasty ruffians, who collect his payments and beat up anyone who gets behind."

"How many?" Marty asked.

"Six that I know of, but maybe more." Mullins replied.

Marty sent a message to the farm after he reunited the girl with her father. She had been beaten before being dumped in the bushes, her assailant had told her if her father didn't pay, she would be raped next time.

Marty was still angry when he got a visit from the de Marchets' the next morning, but he hid it and stored it away. When they left, he changed into some older clothes and armed himself with a full complement of knives and guns.

He was waiting in the study when he heard horses outside the house. The door opened and Tom walked in with his men behind him. Marty shook him by the hand and after a word they went back outside. The boys had brought a spare mount and though they had ridden hard to get there, their horses were still in good shape as they had changed them at the halfway point.

They rode to Bethnal Green. Mullins had given him the address from where the money lender ran his business. Marty ordered them to dismount a short way from the house.

The street was mainly given over to tailor's shops and cloth merchants. Franco was detailed to stay with the horses and the rest walked down to the money lenders.

They were two toughs at the door who were watching them closely as they approached. Marty didn't slow down but just walked up to the nearest one who stepped forward. His foot lashed out kicking him in the left knee and as he started to collapse, he pistol whipped him across the head knocking him unconscious. He looked around and saw a young boy running down the street as if the devil was after him.

Tom had moved almost as fast punching the other tough under the solar plexus and then hitting him with a blackjack.

Marty nodded at the boy.

"Reinforcements will be coming soon. Antton and Matai wait here, any one comes let us know."

Marty opened the door and the four of them entered. A voice called,

"Frankie, who is it?"

Marty signalled to the others and they moved together down the dingy corridor to a room at the back. There were two other doors and Garai and John Smith checked the rooms behind them. There was a thud from Garai's room and a groan. He re-joined them with a grin, held up one finger and crossed his eyes. John came out of his room and just shrugged.

The door in front of Marty opened and a bookish looking man with thinning hair stuck his head out. Marty stepped forward and shouldered the door into the man's body sending him flying backwards.

They entered and there was a flash of light on steel as a big man charged forward swinging what looked like a machete. Marty dove right, out of line and Tom swung a cutlass up in an arc from low to high. There was a scream of agony as it separated the man's hand from his wrist, and the blade, with the hand still clutching it, flew off to the side.

Marty got up and walked over to the bookish man who was in a heap on the floor with the wind knocked out of him. He grabbed him by the collar, dragged him to his feet and pushed him on to a wooden dining room chair. He stepped back and straightened his coat, making sure the now terrified man got a good view of the weapons he carried.

Marty leant forward.

"Mr Goldsmith I presume." He stated; it wasn't a question.

The man started to shake his head, so Marty produced a stiletto from his sleeve and prodded him in the throat. The shake turned to a nod.

Marty pulled up another chair, placed it in front of Goldsmith and sat. He twirled the stiletto between his fingers and the light scintillated off the blade reflecting in bright spots around the walls. There was a noise from the front of the house and Goldsmith suddenly looked sly and cutty eyed. That ended when there was a bang of the door opening and Matai shouted.

"Boss we have company but Antton's got his guns on them."

"Garai, go help those two."

Garai pulled out a pair of pistols and went to the front of the house.

"Now I want to talk to you about the attack on Harold Mullin's daughter, Annabelle, and your dubious business dealings with him." Marty said in a reasonable voice. "I want the name of the man who attacked her."

He waited and when there was no answer he sighed.

"I admire your loyalty, but I fear you may be mistaking me for someone who is reasonable. You see nobody except you and me know we are here, and you don't know who I am. Everyone you can rely on is," he looked at his bodyguard who was huddled in the corner cradling his bleeding arm and moaning, "indisposed. So, I will ask again before I start removing your fingers one by one." He glanced at the stiletto, tutted, put it back into its sheath and pulled out his fighting knife. "There, I always like to use the right tool for the job."

He smiled and Goldsmith suddenly had a dark patch appear at his crutch.

"It was Stevie. I sent Stevie. He were only supposed to frighten her."

Marty nodded to Tom who left and went to join the men at the front and find out who Stevie was.

"Good. Now I'm going to make you an offer," Marty said leaning slightly forward to get Goldsmith's full attention.

"In return for not telling the authorities about your little racket and your, dubious, business practices, you will write off the debt with Mr Mullins. I understand he has already paid off the original capital with interest."

Goldsmith nodded, vigorously.

"I expect there are more unfortunate victims of your greed and I would appeal to your better nature to treat them fairly in future. You see, we can always resume this conversation. I now know where to find you and if you run, someone will know where you have gone. I will always find you," he said with his best wolfish smile.

He looked around as if checking the room was as it should be, stood and the knife disappeared.

"So nice to have done business with you." He smiled and turned to leave. "Oh, I should get him to a surgeon if I were you,' he said in parting as he walked out of the door.

As he left the house he saw that a crowd had gathered. They didn't look particularly threatening and the boys seemed relaxed. Franco was walking the horses up and Garai had a man knelt on the ground with a pistol to the back of his head.

"Stevie?" Marty asked and got a nod in reply.

"Tie his hands in front of him and tether him to one of the horses."

He looked around the crowd and saw some expectant faces.

"Mr Goldsmith is revising his business and from now on will only charge a reasonable amount of interest that will not change while the loan is being paid off. If anyone has a complaint, they can take it to Mr Mullins of Holborn who is a solicitor."

He looked around and saw more smiles.

"Let's go boys."

Chapter 16: Armand Trouble

He was in his study that evening reading the latest news sheet. They had delivered 'Stevie' to the Bow Street Runners and had told Mullins of their 'conversation' with Goldsmith. Annabelle was recovering. He was feeling content.

There was a knock on the front door, and he heard the butler answer it. He looked up expectantly when there was a knock on his study door. The Butler came in and announced. "Mr Wickham, Sir."

Wickham walked in, Marty shook his hand, asked him to sit then ordered coffee and cognac.

Wickham made himself comfortable and lit a cigar. Marty resisted the temptation to frown as he disliked the smell. He was just thankful that he had a fire lit and it drew the smoke away.

Once they had been served and the butler left them alone Wickham took out a packet and tossed it to him. It was sealed with the fouled anchor of the admiralty, so he assumed it was his orders.

"Nothing surprising in there," Wickham stated sipping his coffee.

Marty waited. Wickham didn't deliver documents.

"I hear you were busy this afternoon." Wickham stated as if in passing. Marty wasn't fooled.

"I had the odd errand to run," he replied casually.

"Successfully I hope."

"Yes, thank you."

"Will we find any bodies in the Thames?"

"I don't think so, it was mostly 'armless."

Wickham pondered the burning end of his cigar then said.

"You will have to delay your efforts towards Dieppe for a while."

"Oh, and why is that?"

"Armand has been captured."

Marty froze with his glass halfway to his lips. He absorbed that, then took a sip and put the glass carefully on the table beside him.

"How did he manage that?" he asked trying hard to appear casual.

"It would appear that he decided to get a bit closer to the army encampment to check on something he saw. He overstayed his welcome and was spotted."

"Idiot." Marty swore.

"You need to go and get him out."

Marty didn't answer immediately but thought of all the things that could be extracted from his friend under torture. Armand was strong but nobody could hold out against the professional questioning of the D.I.A. as he had already seen with his friend Jeroen.

"Where is he?"

"They are holding him in Fort Nieulay. It's outside of Calais to the West and controls the river. They built sluices inside the fort to control the flow as part of the defences for the town and port. It is heavily fortified and manned by a full battalion of infantry and a regiment of artillery. It has a substantial curtain wall and a moat."

"Wow! You are full of good news tonight," Marty observed cynically.

"Don't be cheeky." Wickham countered with a half-smile.

"Can you get all the information available on the fort here by tomorrow morning?" Marty asked.

"I have people already gathering it."

There was silence for a few moments.

"You know his wife?" Wickham asked.

"Yes. Susie. She is the daughter of the landlord of the Wagon and Horses. They have a little girl."

"We need to get him back for them." Wickham said gravely.

Marty looked at him and saw worry and compassion in his eyes. Something he never expected.

The next day he turned the dining room into a war room. The information arrived via an anonymous courier who said nothing, just passed Marty the box of papers and left.

The team were all there except James Campbell. They would brief him when they got back.

"Well gentlemen, we need to do a gaol break. Armand has gone and gotten himself arrested."

Various comments greeted that statement, most from the vocabulary of the lower deck and a few choice Basque words as well. Marty let them express themselves and then said.

"Wickham has supplied us with everything known about the fort where he is being kept. Let's go through that first and see where that takes us."

Maps and sketches were shared around but Marty had to read out any documents as he was the only one there who could read properly. He decided there and then that he would try and remedy that in the future.

Their conclusions weren't good. It was a proper fort with good fortifications, fully garrisoned and on the alert. There was only one entrance and that was overlooked by two bastions and could only be approached by a bridge. Any kind of assault was out of the question. That left stealth and deception.

They attacked the problem from every direction imaginable and a few that were just outrageous. In the end they realised there was only one way.

Back at the farm they briefed James and prepared for the trip across to France. They would be taken over by the Deal boys and dropped at Crotoy. From there they would make their way to the road from Amiens to Calais. They had some late intelligence from the old man in Calais that they were sending a squad of cavalry from Paris to pick him up. How he knew that, Marty had no idea, but it all helped as now they had a timescale.

They were all dressed in regular French peasant clothes when they jumped off the boat in Crotoy and were met by Gaston their regular contact. Bad news had travelled fast, and the smugglers knew that Armand had been taken. They offered to help in any way they could.

Marty asked them if they could find out the location of the detachment of soldiers that were coming from Paris. He was well aware that their network could work really fast but was totally unprepared for how quickly they could get word out and information back.

The next morning when they were getting ready to leave, Gaston came in and told them that the soldiers had overnighted in Amiens. Not only that, he reported that there were ten of them plus two officers. There was a cart with a prison cage on the back with two soldiers on it. The other eight were mounted.

Marty was impressed but knew they had to move fast and needed more men.

"No problem my friend, we will accompany you until the soldiers are taken and then some of our men will make up the numbers." Gaston told him. *"We will intercept them at Abbeville."*

Horses were provided and they set out to make the ten-mile trip to the town. It didn't take long as they cantered most of the way knowing they didn't need to save the horses. They arrived well before the soldiers.

They set up an ambush at a checkpoint before the town. They police who normally manned it had been given a large payment by the smugglers to be somewhere else had been and replaced with Antton and Matai.

They had brought over the latest innovation from the Toolshed, as Marty had christened the three inventive marines that manned their workshop at the farm. Crossbows that fired a heavy blunt bolt designed to stun rather than kill. Marty had seen it being tested and knew that if it hit at the base of the skull the victim probably wouldn't survive, but they were quiet and effective. Apart from the crossbows they armed themselves with slings, clubs and blackjacks. They didn't need any unsightly holes in the uniforms.

Anton leaned on the barrier as the detachment arrived. He behaved in the slovenly ill-mannered way that all checkpoint guards did. Matai sat on a chair with his feet up on a table, apparently dozing.

The detachment and their cart plodded up to them. The cart couldn't move faster than a walk over the badly maintained roads. Any faster risked a broken wheel or axle.

The officers rode in the lead and stopped as they got to the barrier.

"You there! Get that thing out of our way!" Ordered one of the officers impatiently. He had a hangover from an extended drinking bout the night before and was even ruder than he normally was.

Antton looked up at him and casually asked him for his papers. The officer bristled but his colleague muttered something to him, and he dug in his pouch and handed over a sheaf of documents. Anton dropped them.

The officer cursed and jumped down off his horse to gather them before the slight morning breeze scattered them. He didn't see the rear rank of men topple off their horses closely followed by the next two. The two on the cart slumped forward and then a mass of men rushed in and pulled the remaining five off their horses. Antton clipped the officer behind the ear with his blackjack and Matai dealt with the other by shooting him the solar plexus with his crossbow. In less than two minutes all the soldiers were overpowered, and their horses secured.

Marty measured himself up against the two officers and chose the uniform that he thought would fit him best. He took the insignia from the other uniform and swapped them for his to make himself the commanding officer. James took the other. The rest of the men changed into the uniforms of the other soldiers. Marty had his team mounted as the escort with five smugglers to make up the numbers. He had two of the smugglers man the cart and the others joined the mounted guards.

Gaston and another man said they would maintained the illusion that the checkpoint was manned until the real ones returned. Marty didn't ask what they were going to do with the soldiers. However, he had a suspicion that an old well nearby would get some use today.

James gathered all the documents and identified the officers. Marty was Captain Hugemont and James was Lieutenant Duval both of the 4th Lancers on detachment to the Department of Internal Affairs. The also had the names of all of the men and the rest took a name each. As the smugglers weren't trained in deception, they just asked them to stay quiet and act surly when they met anyone.

They set off through the town. Most people ignored them; others called out. Local whores offered their wares luridly in screechy voices. One old girl called to him.

"Hey Captain. I bet you've got a big lance! You want to have me polish it for you?"

He waved and smiled at her and she cackled a laugh through half a mouth of teeth.

They left the town after stopping for lunch at a café on the outskirts and made their way on up the road. Their orders said they should overnight in Boulogne, but Marty didn't want to risk a military hostel as too many questions could be asked. So instead they slept in a barn and passed through the town early. They would be at the Fort by midmorning.

The entrance was along a causeway that passed over the moat via a wooden bridge. Marty looked up at the wall and scanned along it to the Bastion on the right. There were twenty-four-pound cannon protruding from the casement at regular intervals. He glanced to the left, it was the same there. He looked over at James and raised his eyebrows.

They passed over the bridge, the horses hooves clattered, the wheels of the cart rumbled, and the gates swung open to let them in. They passed through the maw and tried to keep an even pace. Marty got an itch between his shoulder blades and felt like he was walking into a trap. A sergeant directed them to a block house and when they pulled up outside a Major of Infantry stepped out and waited for Marty to dismount.

"Major Dupont." he greeted them with a casual salute. He had no time or respect for the cavalry, in fact he despised them.

"Captain Hugemont." Marty said urbanely playing the part of the superior cavalryman. Even if he was outranked, he was still superior he told himself as all cavalrymen considered themselves superior to mere infantry. It had something to do with the horses he guessed, being mounted put you above everyone else.

Dupont looked down his nose at him and held out his hand. For a second Marty thought he wanted to shake, but then realised he wanted the papers. He dug into the pouch, pulled out the requisite documents and passed them over. The Major read them and made a gesture towards the blockhouse. A sergeant came out leading two soldiers with Armand suspended between them. He wasn't conscious.

The guards took him around to the back of the cage, threw him in and shut the door. The Major looked smug and said.

"He is all yours. Please sign here that you have received the prisoner."

Marty scribbled an undecipherable signature and said.

"I hope for your sake he lives until Paris. The department wants to question him."

That will make you sweat you bastard.

The Major shrugged.

"He was alive when he left my custody. What happens on the road is your problem."

Marty got back on his horse, flicked a half a salute and wheeled away. He led his men back through the gate and over the wooden bridge without a backward glance. The itch between his shoulder blades got stronger.

Once they got out of sight of the castle he dismounted and rushed to Armand in the cage. He had been badly beaten up and was concussed, but apart from a couple of suspected broken ribs and a hand showing signs of being stamped on, he didn't look too badly damaged. Marty sighed in relief.

"Get him back to Crotoy," he said to James and passed him the pouch.

"Tell Gaston I have things to do in Calais. I will be at the meeting point at Wissant, at dusk, three days from now," he told the senior smuggler.

He stripped of his uniform, handed it to James and put on the clothes he had worn on the trip over.

"I need to find the information Armand was collecting and find out what made him risk capture." Marty told James. "Get him home to his wife and child."

James nodded but looked like he would rather stay.

"If anybody questions where the captain is, tell them he got sick and your orders didn't allow for any delay, so you left him behind at his order. Now go."

Marty took off on foot, a French civilian riding a cavalry horse would be very suspicious and made his way to the house that Armand had been using. He knocked at the door and this time the old man practically dragged him inside.

"Have you gotten him out?" he asked, visibly distressed.

"Don't worry he is safe. A little beaten up but otherwise fine. He is on his way home." Marty reassured him.

"Thank God! I thought they were going to shoot him." The old man had tears in his eyes.

"What is your name?" Marty asked him.

"Francois Legrande at your service. I was one of Monsieur Armand's family retainers before the revolution," he replied recovering his composure.

"I am Martin and I need your help to complete Armand's mission."

"I will help in any way I can Sir." Francois offered.

Marty quizzed him on what Armand was doing and what he found prior to his disastrous sortie into the camp and then asked him to show him Armand's room. If he had made any notes they would be in there.

The room was quite large and had a nice bed, a wardrobe and a dressing table. First, he searched the room in general, looking under the bed and around the inside of the wardrobe. Then he pulled the drawers completely out from the dressing table and checked inside the recess and under the base of the drawers themselves.

Nothing.

He stopped and walked to the centre of the room and just looked. Slowly turning in a circle. He was trying to think like Armand. There was a fireplace. He checked the chimney, nothing. He sat back and looked carefully at the brickwork at the back of the fire. He scanned each row and then he noticed that one brick sat slightly further back than the others. He looked closer and saw two very small gaps in the mortar either end of the brick.

Now what goes in there? he thought. He stood and went back to the dressing table. It had been used by a lady in days gone by and there was a stand with button hooks on it. Marty picked up each hook in turn and ran his finger and thumb down the shafts. Two left a very slight black mark.

He returned to the fireplace and very carefully inserted the hooks into the two slots as far as he could then turned them ninety degrees and gently pulled. The brick slid out and before it could drop on the floor, he carefully held it by pressing his fingers against the ends and pulled it out all the way. He made extra sure that he put it down with the outward side facing upwards so it wouldn't get damaged.

Now he could see into the cavity and at the back were some rolled up papers which he carefully retrieved.

He recognised the writing as Armand's, but they were in code. *This is going to take a while,* he thought.

After working half the night, he had deciphered the papers. Most of what they held was numbers of troops, horses and so on, but one had a description of what Armand called a 'ballon de transport' or transport balloon. It apparently could carry ten men and would, Armand suspected, be towed behind a vessel of some kind.

Marty sat and thought about it. If all the barges had a balloon tied to them that would increase their carrying capacity by a third! Or they could carry stores or horses in the barges and the men in the balloons.

This was serious, Marty had read that Jacques Charles and Robert Brothers had made "La Caroline" an elongated, steerable craft that had internal gas cells, a rudder and something that pushed it along. Jean Baptiste Meusnier, the French Revolutionary General had championed it in 1784. So, he could quite believe this was feasible. He read the paper again and noticed that it said that the balloons relied on a gas to make them fly. It also said that the gas was highly inflammable. The part of Marty's soul that was an arsonist started to speak to him.

He burnt his decoded versions making sure there wasn't a scrap left and returned the originals to the cavity in the fire place. He carefully replaced the brick, but this time made sure that it was level with its counterparts either side.

He slept for four hours and woke refreshed and had a hearty breakfast of cheese and ham with croissant, which he loved, washed down with strong coffee. It was time to go and look for those cargo balloons.

It was just getting light when he arrived at the perimeter of the army encampment. He had chosen an entry point close to the powder store that was marked on a hand drawn map in Armand's notes. He started to crawl across the dew drenched grass, getting thoroughly soaked in the process. He looked back. *Oh shit!* He thought as his trail was clearly visible as a dark line across the dew-covered field.

He had no option, he backtracked down the same line until he came to the ditch he had started at. He made his way along to a gravel path and took that at a stroll hoping no one would challenge him.

He got lucky and came across a civilian working party that was loading a cart with casks of powder from a powder store. He joined in and helped load a couple of casks before he slipped behind a stack and waited for them to move off. Once all was quiet, he used his knife to remove the bung from one of the casks and check the contents. It was artillery grade gunpowder. He looked around and found a smaller cask which provided some fine ground priming powder.

Humming quietly to himself he took a brass timer out of his pocket, wound up the wheel lock and set it. He then selected a cask of powder in the middle of a stack and, after removing the bung, poured a good portion of priming powder into it. Finally, he set the timer to twenty, *too short*, forty minutes and lodged it in the bung hole with a rag wrapped around it so the wheel lock was directly above the priming powder. It was precisely nine o'clock in the morning according to his watch. Satisfied he made his way to the entrance.

There was a guard outside who had a sudden urge to sleep as Marty's blackjack sang him a lullaby. He was found a comfortable spot, out of sight, where he could slumber undisturbed, trussed up and gagged.

Marty checked the map and made off in the direction of the balloon storage. He joined another civilian group that were moving in the right direction and left them when they turned towards the food tents.

He ducked into a tent, as there were a number of soldiers heading straight at him, to be confronted with the sight of a whorehouse. There were half naked girls sprawled around eating croissant and a couple of officers doing up their uniforms getting ready to leave. The madam swore at him as this was an officer only establishment and a bouncer ejected him through the tent flap with a hearty shove.

He landed in the dirt outside of the tent much to the amusement of the soldiers he had ducked inside to avoid. They called out ribald suggestions and insults at random as they marched by.

He stood and brushed himself off with a show of injured dignity then carried on walking in the direction of the balloon store.

He spotted a sign outside a compound that with big red letters and a pictogram of an explosion warned of 'Inflammable Gas'. He stopped and looked around, there was one man inside that he could see. He was a scholarly looking fellow with a shaggy mane of brown hair that looked to be totally out of control and had a pair of round glasses perched on his nose.

The man looked up, noticed him and said, *"You are here at last! You are late! Get in here and assist me immediately."*

Marty hesitated for about a count of three and then hurried into the compound. The man started giving him rapid instructions, obviously expecting him to understand what he meant and when Marty didn't respond as expected peered at him closely.

"You aren't de Jorney! Who are you? What are you doing here?"

He was about to ask yet another question when Marty punched him on the jaw, knocking him out.

"I dunno who de Jorney is," he muttered as he moved the man behind a pile of boxes, "but I bet he knows where he is better off."

There was a contraption under a canvas roof in the centre of the compound and Marty went to look at it. It looked like a large kettle of some kind. The spout had a canvas pipe connected to a large bladder held under a cargo net that was staked to the ground. The bladder looked to be about half full. There were a lot of boxes with iron filings nearby and demi-johns with the skull and crossbones for poison on them. He carefully un-stoppered one of the demi-johns and recoiled at the smell of sulphur that almost burnt the hair out of his nose.

After thinking about what the now unconscious man had told him to do, he took the lid off the kettle and dumped in a box full of iron filings and then took a demi-john of brimstone smelling liquid and poured that in on top. The reaction was immediate, it started to bubble. He clamped the lid back on.

He looked at his watch, thirty minutes had passed since he set the timer!

He heard a noise and glanced over his shoulder. The bladder was inflating! Whatever the kettle was producing was being forced into the bladder!

He stood and thought for a moment. *If that kettle thing is making the gas to raise the balloons, then whatever is in that bladder is inflammable or maybe even explosive according to Armond's notes.*

He could feel a fire coming on.

He glanced at his watch.

Four minutes to go.

He went to the bladder and cut a small slit in it near to the pipe that joined it to the kettle. Not big enough to stop the inflation but big enough to let out a steady stream of gas. He had one more timer in his pocket which he took out, set the wheel lock and wound the setting to six minutes. He carefully placed the timer by the stream of gas escaping from the slit he had cut.

He found the scholarly man, slung him over his shoulder and carried him out of the compound. He was spotted by a guard who was just about to challenge him when the powder store exploded. They felt the concussion where they stood, and the guard looked in horror at the mushroom cloud of smoke that was drifting into the sky. *Twenty plus tons of black powder sure makes a significant bang.* Marty thought with a grin and broke into a run.

There was a whole load of secondary explosions as kegs were thrown in the air and detonated. It was a very impressive display that flattened everything near it. But if he was right in his assumption about the gas, he needed to get away from the immediate area as soon as possible, so he yelled to the guard to follow him and ran towards the burning powder store. He stopped by the brothel to deposit his passenger into the caring arms of a pair of whores who he tossed a silver half Louis to.

As he turned away there was a whoosh as the gas from the leak he had created ignited. The bladder was slightly porous to hydrogen so there was a thin layer of the gas all around it which ignited as well. The heat caused the bladder to rupture from where he had cut the slit and it exploded with a sharp, very loud, bang. The blast sprayed sulphuric acid everywhere in a hundred-yard radius. It was time to leave.

Chapter 17: Barging around

Marty had no trouble leaving the camp. He just joined a group of fleeing civilians, ducking out of the group as they got to the town. There was quite a crowd gathered on the outskirts watching the smoke rising from the direction of the encampment, but he didn't want to wait there.

He wandered back to the house, checking his back trail regularly to make sure he wasn't followed. Once he got there he went straight to Armand's room, retrieved the documents from the fireplace and collected Armand's personal belongings. He said goodbye to Francoise with a promise to let him know how Armand was and left.

It took him the whole day to make the ten-mile trip to Wissant because he had to avoid all the checkpoints on the way. He trekked through ditches, pushed through hedges and wadded across streams. By the time he got there he was tired and thoroughly fed up.

He hid out in the dunes until dusk and a fishing boat appeared with a red light over a white. It was time to go home.

Back at Deal he paid a visit to Armand, Susie and their daughter and spent the day with them, catching up. Armand was on rest leave to recover from the beating he had taken, and Marty wanted to check up on his friend, and to ask him if there was anything extra to his notes that he wanted to add to the report. There were a couple of things but in the main they drank wine, ate Susie's pies and played with the baby.

Marty turned his mind back to his orders concerning Dieppe once he got back to the farm. He needed to source a couple of sailing barges. He took a trip in the Lark down the coast to Dorset and had a chat with a couple of barge operators in a bar in Poole. They told him about an old boy in Weymouth who had a couple of barges, who was too old to run them now and his sons weren't interested in continuing the family business.

They moored up at the quay and Marty asked where to find Matthew Fitch. He was told he needed to go up river a way, he would know when they'd gone far enough when they saw the barges. Marty got the ship's boat manned and they rowed him upstream. Clear of the town and just as they entered Radipole Lake he saw a pair of barges moored up at wooden dock on the west shore. They pulled over and Marty climbed up on the dock and called out.

"AHOY MR FITCH!"

An old man about five feet four tall came out of a house at the end of the dock and walked with a sailor's roll towards him. His legs were so bandy he couldn't stop a pig in a poke! The old boy had huge forearms, biceps and shoulders. Testimony to the hard life of a bargeman, hauling on tackles to load and unload heavy cargo and hauling up sails with just the minimum number of hands that they could get away with.

"What can I do fer you sor?" he asked, his Dorset accent pronounced.

"Well I heard that thee were lookin' to get rid o' these barges of yourn." Marty drawled back at him.

The old boy looked at him and the uniform and asked.

"Where be ye from son?"

"I be born in Arne on the Frome," Marty replied.

"Purbeck family?"

"Surely. I be Martin Stockley." Martin introduced himself and held out his hand which old man Fitch took and shook warmly.

"You had a relative called Cecil? Worked the mines at Worth Matravers?"

"Yea, he were my uncle. Bin dead now ten year since." Marty told him.

"Ay I 'eard. He were a friend o' mine back when."

The old boy looked at Marty closely.

"You 'ave is look abou' yer. Now what kin I do fer ya?"

"I be in need of a couple of barges and I 'eard that yer were lookin' to get rid o' yourn." Marty told him.

Old Fitch looked at him and over at the boat. He scanned an expert eye over the crew and then at Marty.

"Now what do a Navy man want with a working man's boat?" he asked.

"I honestly caint tell yer tha' as it be Navy business," Marty explained, "but I can say it will help us deal a proper smack in the chops to old Bony."

The old boy got a shrewd cutty look to his eyes and opened the bargaining.

"Forty quid each." He stated, spat on his palm and held it out.

Marty knew this game as he'd been with his father and uncles when they had bargained. He also knew that the two old barges were not worth that.

"I needs to cast me eye over 'em afore we start that," he laughed.

The old boy grinned at that. He was happy his first impression of Marty had been right. He had figured the boy was no fool and would be as smart as his old friend Cecil. He had looked him over as he had walked up to him and seen the well-muscled frame and confident stance. He had recognized him immediately as the family resemblance was startling. *He and Cecil could be brothers.* He thought as he watched him go over the first barge.

He was surprised when he called a big tattooed man with a broken nose out of the boat. While Martin was obviously the officer, he treated the man with a lot of respect and asked his opinion in an accent decidedly different from the one he used when talking to him. *'His Navy voice I s'pose,"* he thought. There was also a familiarity between them that told him these two had been through a lot together.

Marty took off his jacket and he saw the large knife on the back of his belt, he looked closer and saw another knife in his boot. Marty handed the jacket to the big man who he heard him call Tom. He could tell by the way it hung that there was something heavy in the pockets. *'An' I bet it aint just gold coins.'*

The boy was down in the bilges of the barge and when he came up he had the big knife in his hand. The blade caught the light and he could see the patterned steel. *'A beautiful piece of work'.*

He suddenly remembered something he had heard in the pub about a boy from over Corfe way that had done well in the Navy and had married some titled woman from up north. He wondered if this was the same one. He would have quite a yarn to tell if it were. He could drink out for free on that for months!

Marty finished his inspection and with Tom concluded that the barges were well worn, old, but still sound and serviceable. He asked Tom what he thought they were worth, and he laughed and just said. "What yer pay for them." *'Very helpful,'* he thought.

He walked back up the dock to where old Fitch was stood watching him. He saw he was looking at him speculatively and wondered what the old boy was thinking.

"Ye said forty each?" Marty asked.

"Tha' be where I be." Fitch answered.

"Fifteen each." Marty said, spit on his hand and held it out.

'Cheeky young pup!' Fitch thought but spit on his own hand and said.

"Thirty-five!" He grabbed Marty's right wrist with his left hand and slapped his palm.

"Twenty!" Marty countered and returned the compliment.

"Thirty!" Fitch came back.

"Twenty-five!"

"Twenty-eight!" Fitch held his wrist and when he slapped his palm, he left it touching.

Marty looked at him and grinned.

"Done!" he said and closed his hand on Fitch's.

They shook.

Marty took his jacket back from Tom and dug into one of his pockets. He pulled out a barker and then a pouch.

Fitch raised his eyebrows at the gun but was more interested in the pouch.

Marty took him over to a table on the porch of his house and sat down. Fitch sat opposite him. Marty poured the contents of the pouch onto the table. There was a cascade of silver guineas. Marty counted out fifty-six and pushed them across to Fitch who raised his eyebrows in question.

"You been straight, and you were a friend of my uncle Cecil." Marty said. "The Navy pays in guineas. That's twenty-one shillin' to the pound. Let's call it a bonus."

Fitch thanked him and then gave him a straight look.

"Be you the boy I heard about who wed the lass from up north?" he asked.

"Aye, that would be me," Marty admitted.

"Be she as beautiful as they all said?"

"You be asking the wrong man, I have a biased view on that particular subject, but I would say she be even more beautiful, and our kids are as well."

Old Fitch laughed and looked at Tom who grinned and nodded.

They both stood.

"Will you be safe with that much cash lying around here?" Marty asked.

"I be fine. Anyone unwelcome who be visiting will get a hot welcome from old Bess." Fitch responded nodding to the biggest blunderbuss Marty had ever seen propped up by the door with the hammer at half cock.

"Sides it will be stowed away where no bugger but me will find it as soon as you shove off."

Marty shook his hand and walked down to his boat.

"I'll have a couple of crews here before the end of next week to pick them up. Mind you don't shoot them!" he called in parting.

Once back on the boat he sailed around to one of the docks where they loaded barges with stone near Winspit Quarry, which was half way between Weymouth and Swanage. They tied up and Marty went ashore. He talked to the owners and explained what he wanted. They were more than happy for him to take the rubbish and they agreed just a loading price for the time their men would use. They even agreed to mix mortar and pour that in on top once Marty explained that the barges would be scuttled to block a French harbour.

Marty went back to the farm and started organising crews and planning routes. He decided to put the two midshipmen in charge of the barges with eight-man crews. He would take them down on the Swan and escort them up to Winspit where they would load.

He then had a choice, he could either have them cross the channel directly from Swanage to Cherbourg, a distance of some sixty-six miles, and follow the French coast East past Normandy to Dieppe, or sail up the English coast to around Dungeness and cross over North of Boulogne, a distance of just twenty-five miles, and then south down the French coast to Dieppe.

The crossing was the dangerous part. The barges would be heavily laden and if the sea got up, they could be swamped. It was late in the year and the weather, while fine at the moment could turn in a moment. In the end he decided discretion was the better part of valour and opted for the longer trip up the English coast and across the narrower part of the Channel.

The plan was simple in the end. Pick up the barges, fill them with stone and then mortar, sail them up the coast to Dungeness, cross the channel to the point north of Audressells and sail south to Dieppe. Scuttle them and run home victorious.

What he didn't know and never could have known was that down in the Caribbean a storm was brewing. It was just a child in the Atlantic south west of Trinidad, but it was growing fast and as it grew it tightened in on itself and got stronger. It gathered energy and moved Northwest up the islands causing death and destruction wherever it touched. It came to adulthood just to the North of Cuba. Its winds hit almost one-hundred miles an hour and shoved a wall of water along in front of it.

It turned and visited the coast of the Carolinas, decimating fishing ports and any buildings within ten miles of the coast. Then it turned Northwest out into the Atlantic and matured into a tropical storm. It had its eye focused on a landfall at the Lizard.

The S.O.F, meantime, continued to prepare for Operation Dam as they named it. Marty ferried the crews down to Weymouth and had them prepare the barges. Once they were ready, they moved them down into Weymouth Harbour and then up the coast to the quarry. It took a week to load them with stone and another week to make mortar and pour it into the holds. They were lucky that the quarrymen had pre-prepared the lime putty from quicklime before they got there, or they would have been there a month.

The trip up the coast to Dungeness was slow. The barges couldn't handle anything over a moderate sea so as soon as it picked up, they had to find shelter somewhere. At least they knew their cargo wouldn't shift, but in the end, it took two weeks to get to the point where they would make the crossing.

The weather looked fine as they started but around half way across the waves started to grow. The barges were only making three or four knots at best and the sea was coming in on the beam. Marty fretted and had to put the Alouette under minimum sail to stay with them. The crews on the barges were having a horrible time of it their flat bottoms didn't help at all.

They had the Leeboards down but were still making about as much leeway as they were heading for the last three hours of the crossing and they made landfall closer to Calais than the point at Audressells. Marty recognised Wissant and they decided to moor up in the bay for the night.

The next morning dawned fair. The wind had dropped and was more from the West. Marty got them under sail again and they headed South. They had about seventy-five miles to go.

They flew French colours and Marty stood The Alouette off, as it would look strange for barges to be escorted by a corvette. He stayed close enough that he could keep an eye on them and run interference if anybody tried to interfere with them be they French or British.

The wind continued to increase as they turned South around the point and headed down the coast past Boulogne. Now the waves were coming in from the west and increasing as well. The storm was reaching the Lizard and shoving a wall of water in front of it which was being channelled into the English Channel causing a storm surge. The wind was now veering to the North as the edge of the storms effect was starting to be felt. All of that added up to wind against tide and one confused sea.

Marty looked to the west and could see the dark swirling clouds on the horizon, they were moving in fast. He made the decision that they would all have to take shelter and the closest he knew of was Le Touquet where they could at least anchor in the inlet. He steered in towards the barges and raised a signal spelling out 'anchor Touquet' he got acknowledgements from both of them.

They got into the estuary, worked their way in to where they thought they would be safe and dropped anchor. They weren't far from the boatyards they had burnt earlier that year and Marty thought he could still smell the burnt remnants. Marty ordered a stern anchor run out as well for The Alouette and thought that would be enough. They were set facing upstream to the East.

The sky got darker and darker. Soon it was as if night had fallen in the middle of the day. The wind started to shriek through the rigging from the North and the pennant was a stiff iron bar. The crew huddled below and only a minimum watch was kept.

Marty couldn't believe it, but the wind got even stronger and the ship was canted over as the gale pushed against her rigging from the side and he could hear the creak of the stern anchor cable that ran out from above his cabin. He put on his coat and went up on deck. If he were a religious man, he would have thought that Armageddon was on its way. The sky was black, and the waves were coming into the estuary and hitting his ship on the stern.

He looked at the shore and was shocked to see that the water level had risen to the point it was lapping against the top of the slips in the boat yards. He called the hands, they needed to let some slack out into the anchor cables, or they would start to drag. He ran forward and tried to see the barges. He could see one but not the other. He hoped it was just further upstream and obscured by the other one.

The ship eased a bit as they let out some cable, but the wind just kept increasing and was swinging rapidly from North towards the West. The Alouette was at odds with the wind and the sea. The sea trying to get her keel to go one way and the wind pushing her upper works the other.

There was a load bang and Marty froze, feeling through his legs for any unusual movement. Then he saw one of the lookouts waving at him from up forward. He fought his way to the foremast and the man cupped his hands and shouted.

"The barge's aft anchor cable parted! She is swinging towards shore!"

Marty ran to the rail and could just see the barge swinging away from the wind held only by her bow anchor. As he watched he could see that she was slipping closer to the shore. There was movement on her decks as her crew were trying to use sweeps to pull her away, but she was too heavy, the wind was too strong, and she swung around so her stern was almost rubbing the bank.

The wind continued to swing around the compass from North to West and then South which was testament to how strong and concentrated the storm was. The worrying thing was that the barge stopped swinging with her stern against the bank. Marty watched while its crew frantically pushed with poles against the bank trying to get her to move. It looked like that she was well aground.

The water level hadn't gotten any higher and the storm was still raging after it got dark. All they could do was sit tight and wait for it to pass. Marty didn't sleep and when it got light, he could see that The Alouette had dragged her stern anchor during the night. The water level was much lower, and he could see that the barge nearest them had her stern high and dry on the bank.

He got his gig to take him over and boarded her. He was greeted by a disconsolate Midshipman Campbell who looked absolutely exhausted.

"We tried everything Sir," he all but sobbed. "She got hung up on the bank and was too heavy for us to move."

Marty went to have a look and it was obvious that the barge was going nowhere. He crossed to the starboard side and looked for the other barge. It was most noticeable by its absence.

There was only one thing to do and that was to get back in the boat and go and look for it. He was concerned for his men most of all, after that for the mission. They headed upstream past the stricken barge and further up the river, which was navigable all the way up to Etaples, but looking ahead he couldn't see the barge anywhere. The rounded a shallow curve and there was a shout from the North bank. Marty looked and could see Midshipman Thompson and six men stood on the bank waving their arms.

Tom steered the gig over and they threw them a mooring rope so Marty could scramble ashore.

"Well, where is my barge and two of your men?" he asked Thompson.

"My apologies Sir, but the barge is sunk in the middle of the channel over there," he said and pointed to a spot about halfway across the river.

"Her anchor broke loose in the night and we were pushed upstream on the flood. I think we hit a tree or something large floating on the water which stove in a couple of planks at the bow. She went down in a few minutes. We all got off and swam over here but it turns out Miller and Davies couldn't swim, and I couldn't find them in the dark."

He looked so wretched that Marty relented and patted him on the shoulder, after Thompson had pointed it out he could see the mast sticking up around mid-channel a little way up stream.

"Look, you did what you could, and no one can blame you for losing a couple of men in that maelstrom last night." He looked at the other men. "Get in the gig we need to go home."

The wind was contrary, so they used the sweeps to get The Alouette out of the estuary once the wind had dropped to the point, they could row against it. It was a hard slog and all of the rowers were exhausted by the time they had enough sea room to hoist the sails. Marty looked back at the plume of smoke from the burning barge and sighed.

Chapter 18 Truth and Consequences

He sent in his report and waited for the bad news. Officers who failed in their missions had to face a court-martial and his had gone spectacularly wrong. On top of that he had lost two men for no noticeable gain. Caroline was in Cheshire sorting out a problem on the estate. A pair of tenants were disputing the rights to grazing on some land that for some reason had never been formally enclosed between their tenancies. Armand was staying at the farm and tried to reassure Marty that he had done nothing wrong, but it didn't stop him from fretting and stressing over it.

The dreaded letter arrived, Marty was summoned to attend a court-martial inquiry into the loss of the two barges and the failure of his mission. It was to be held in the port of London at St Catherine's dock on the frigate, HMS Tempest. It didn't strike him as unusual, but it was probably the first and last to be held there especially as St Catherine's was a commercial dock.

He reported aboard at the allotted time and was shown in to the captain's cabin. There was the usual table with four officers and a clerk sat behind it. In the middle was Commodore Pellew, with three other Captains whose names just slid over him but were all familiar in some way. He welcomed Marty and made an opening statement.

"We are not here to try you for dereliction of duty or to judge you. We are here to establish the facts of what has occurred and make a recommendation as to what further action, if any, should be taken. Do you understand?"

Marty confirmed his understanding and the enquiry began. They had his report and also reports from the two Midshipmen. They asked him to describe the entire mission from its planning through to the aborted end. He was cross examined and asked to justify his decisions. When they had finished, he was told he would be informed of the outcome at the Admiralties convenience.

As he left, he looked through to the coach and saw both his midshipmen sitting pale faced, waiting to be called. He wanted to reassure them but the lieutenant escorting him hurried him along and off the ship.

He stood on the harbour and looked at the ship for the first time. She was an old 'Jackass Frigate'. Too small to be of much use against the modern French frigates but too big to be considered a Sloop and had a raised quarterdeck. She was probably twenty years old but looked to be in fair condition. *'What the hell is she doing here?'* he thought.

Puzzled he left the docks and got a cab to his house. Blaez met him at the door, letting him know that he was upset at being left out of whatever his boss had been doing. After he got out of uniform, he went into the drawing room and sat in his favourite chair. Blaez climbed on his lap and made himself comfortable. He had this neat trick of leaning back with his head stretched up so that the top of it was laying against Marty's chest and licking him under the chin. Marty was expected to rub his throat and make 'love you' noises. He wished Caroline was there. He could do with a cuddle right now and was feeling vulnerable.

He heard nothing from the Admiralty for a week. Both James Campbell and Ryan Thompson visited but all they could tell him was that they had been interrogated, just as he was.

Caroline came back to London at the weekend and life was better. He wondered why he had heard nothing from either Hood or Wickham. Even Armand seemed to be avoiding him. He was just beginning to feel like an outcast when a courier arrived at breakfast on the Monday morning with a letter from the admiralty.

He opened it with his heart in his mouth and his stomach knotted. His hands shook for the first time ever, he was genuinely frightened at what he would read.

Caroline watched as he opened the envelope and took out the paper inside. She tried to read his expression as he scanned down the page. She was scared for him too but at the same time had a guilty wish he was kicked out of the Navy so she could keep him to herself. He looked at her and folded onto his chair.

"What does it say?" she asked with her heart in her mouth.

Marty took a deep shuddering breath.

"I have been exonerated of any blame, and neither I nor my Midshipmen will face any further action."

He started to laugh and then jumped out of his chair, grabbed Caroline and swung her around. She squealed and found herself being kissed very thoroughly then picked up and carried upstairs.

Wickham came visiting the next morning and, once he had settled in one of the comfortable chairs in the library with a cup of coffee, said.

"Armand will not be going back into France again, the beating he received had permanently damaged his ribs."

"Will he be forced out of the Navy as well?" Marty asked.

"No, he will retain his rank and take over the SOF operation in Deal. He will also be handling some of our agents in France and being in Deal at The Farm will make that easy."

Marty suddenly realised what that meant was, he wasn't going to be in command of the S.O.F. anymore. Was his career over?

Wickham continued.

"He will be able to be with his wife and child as well. He deserves that. Had the pleasure of meeting his good lady last week actually. Makes a damn fine pie!"

Marty swallowed and agreed with a forced smile.

"Oh, and Linette is back in England as well. She said to say hello and to give you her love." He leaned forward conspiratorially. "How close did you two actually work together in France?"

Marty's face must have shown his outrage at the idea and Wickham chuckled and said.

"Oh don't look like that she told me it was all very professional and in any case she likes Caroline too much to . . . well you know," he finished lamely.

Marty was feeling like he was going to explode! When would this damn man put him out of his misery!

There was a knock at the front door, and he heard the butler greet whoever it was. The library door opened, the butler entered and announced:

"Admiral Lord Hood, Milord," and in walked Hood with a beaming smile on his face.

"Martin m'boy! How are you?" he roared in his quarterdeck voice. "Is that coffee? Capital, capital. Sorry I'm late."

Now Marty was totally confused, he had just been told news that was completely at odds with the welcome from Hood. He composed himself as Hood was served coffee and the Butler discreetly made himself scarce.

"To business." Hood opened. "I believe William has told you about Armand?"

Marty nodded.

"Good. Now we have a problem," he continued, and Marty thought '*here it comes!*'

"Our holdings in the Caribbean are being badly affected by the depredations of privateers and pirates." Hood started to explain

'What the hell?' Marty thought but just managed to keep a straight face.

"They are taking any cargo vessel that's not in convoy and escorted by the Navy and even then, the audacious bastards are cutting ships out of the convoys before our boys can stop them. The Caribbean fleet doesn't have enough ships to patrol all the islands, or properly escort the convoys, and really is on a hiding to nothing. We are losing millions of pounds because of it."

'By 'we' he means the plantation owners and Lloyds I bet.'

"You, my boy, have an enviable record against pirates, don't you?" It was a rhetorical question, but Marty nodded all the same.

"So, what we want you to do is pose as a privateer, or pirate, and infiltrate the pirate brotherhood so we can pinpoint their bases and hit them at home as it were." He then leaned back in his chair with his coffee and beamed at Marty expectantly.

"You have a plan already?" Marty asked.

"No, we thought as you are the expert, we would leave that to you," Wickham chipped in.

"We do have a ship for you. She was coming up for decommissioning and was sold off yesterday, so we took the liberty of buying her in your name," Hood smiled.

'What are they going to be lumbering me with?' Marty thought worriedly.

"In fact, you know her. It's the Tempest."

"The Frigate that my enquiry was held on?"

"The very one!"

Marty had a sudden realisation.

"My 'inquiry' was a put-up job?" He asked through clenched teeth.

"The enquiry was absolutely genuine." Hood placated him. "The result, however, was never in doubt."

"You mean I have been sitting here for the last week, chewing my fingernails to the quick worrying about the outcome for nothing?" Marty fairly squawked, outraged.

The two older men looked at each other in amazement.

"You didn't twig it?" Wickham asked. "The ship being in a commercial dock in London. Pellew, who was on your commissioning board as chairman. Three Captains who all had served under Hood."

"It was rigged?" Marty stated glaring at the two of them.

"Well rigged is maybe putting it too strongly." Wickham stated trying to placate him. "The enquiry was genuine enough."

Marty took a deep breath and let it out slowly. *'His record was clean and that was all that mattered in the end,'* he told himself.

"On paper I own The Tempest?" he asked trying to get things back on track.

"Well a man called Martin Stanwell does and that is in fact you." Hood answered relieved the fire had been damped down.

"My Nom de plume then. My crew?" Marty asked.

"Apart from the rogues who follow you around and James Campbell you need to recruit a crew. We think that the pirates have eyes in London and other main ports so we need to make this look as genuine as we can." Hood clarified.

Marty considered for a moment or two then said.

"Alright it can be done. It's November now and the end of the Hurricane season. To get a full crew together around a core of men I can trust will take at least a couple of months as will fitting out the Tempest as a privateer. I will aim to sail in early March."

He looked at the two of them.

"I want the crew of the Lark and twenty of the Marines from the S.O.F.. I assume this is being done under the auspices of the S.O.F.?"

"Absolutely," said Hood without batting an eyelid. "You can have your men."

The two men walked side by side back to Wickham's house.

"You changed your mind then." Wickham stated. "This will be an S.O.F. operation after all."

"Naval Intelligence or S.O.F. what's the difference?" Hood pondered. "Either way he is on his own once he is out there. Nobody is going to run to his rescue if he gets into a mess, but that is nothing new. If he manages this, there will be a Captaincy in it for him." Hood replied.

"Well that won't make any difference to the Navy." Wickham chuckled. "Half the Captains are bloody pirates all ready."

Chapter 19:   The Tempest

"Sorry love but this time you can't come with me." Marty told Caroline when he broke the news of his new mission to her. "I won't be on any of the main islands and I wouldn't sleep at night knowing you were out there with the kids exposed to all the fevers and the like."

The look on her face told him she didn't like the idea – at all. She was about to protest when she looked at the pile of letters on her desk and thought about running her (their) commercial empire from the Caribbean. She had fingers in a lot of pies these days including the estates in Cheshire and Dorset, the wine and brandy distribution business, importing gem stones and spices, the shipping company and a number of other things she didn't think Marty knew about yet.

She had thoughts about maybe acquiring a plantation or two when she heard he was going to be in the Caribbean, but that could wait, as she suspected there would be some fallout from this latest mission and knowing Marty she expected that he would come out of it with something substantial.

She capitulated much to Marty's surprise and even though there was a slight mist of suspicion in his mind he accepted it at face value.

"I need to get down to St Catherine's dock and start getting The Tempest into shape," he said. "I will be back for dinner and to put the kids to bed."

He had started dressing in the typical clothes of a Privateer. A frilled shirt and long black jacket, tight fitting breaches and high boots. He was armed as usual and got some interested stares from dock workers and some interesting offers from the whores hanging out of their windows. He was deeply into his alter ego's persona and his language was reverting more to Dorset than the Navy.

The Tempest stood high in the water. The Navy had stripped her of her guns, but Marty didn't mind that at all. He was meeting Tom and they would work out what they needed then go and talk to his old friend Mr Fletcher, who he knew could outfit his ship just how he wanted it.

She was tied up at the dock and Marty saw that the Shadows were already onboard along with James. The rest of the Snipes would arrive in the next couple of days along with the twenty named marines he had chosen. He approached the gangplank and found himself looking down the barrel of a pistol until Antton realised it was him and beckoned him aboard with a laugh.

"Is that necessary?" he asked nodding at the pistol.

"This dock is full of thievin' 'erberts." John Smith supplied as he walked past with a box of fresh vegetables. "Caught one trying to shin up the forward mooring rope last night."

"Did you now, and what happened to him?" Marty asked.

"*She* ended up swimmin' back to shore." John laughed.

He was soon joined by Tom and James and they walked the gun deck. She was set up to carry twenty-four guns and had nine-pounders fitted before. She had no stern chasers but could be fitted with a couple of fore chasers. At the moment she had ports for twelve guns a side, but Marty had ideas about that.

"If we put in a couple of big fore chasers how many ports would we have to lose?" he asked Tom.

"What like long nines? Or bigger?" Tom asked.

"I was thinking twenty-four pounders." Marty replied.

"Then you would lose two at the front each side." Tom calculated. "If you be plannin' on adding a couple of carronades a side at the stern you would probably maintain her trim an' all. An' if you mount the rearmost pair in the aft corner of the quarterdeck you could train them around to cover the stern."

"If you made the guns on the side twelve pounders would you still get ten in." James asked.

Marty laughed as James had read his mind.

"She be broad in the beam," Tom observed, "so I reckon she could take 'em."

A voice made them jump.

"And make sure there are plenty of mounts for swivels down the rails and all," said the urbane tones of Paul La Pierre, the Marine Lieutenant.

"What are you doing here?" Marty asked in surprise.

"Heard you were up to something and as things are quiet at the farm thought I'd come along and offer m' services."

"No raids?" Marty asked.

"Just smashing up semaphore towers and the like, unfortunately Armand hasn't got your imagination and they don't need me for that," he looked around "but this looks much more interesting. Where are we going?"

Marty noted the 'we' in that question and couldn't help but smile.

"Well if you are determined to tag along, we are heading down to the Caribbean to play pirate for a bit."

"Sounds, bloody marvellous." Paul grinned back at him "I'll get my stuff aboard then."

Two days later Marty and Tom were sat drinking a glass of port in Fletcher's office. He had his manservant replace the short-legged chair, that he had tried to intimidate Marty in last time he was there, with a couple of nice padded chairs. He did however keep a careful eye on the saddlebags that Marty dropped beside his seat with a pronounced clink.

"You are shopping again I hear," he mentioned with a sly look. "Need to fill up something a bit bigger this time."

"You are well informed as usual." Marty smiled back. "Word gets around doesn't it."

"Don't worry, nobody else made the connection between the sale of the Frigate and you." Fletcher reassured him. "Now what do you need?"

Marty handed over the list and Fletcher went to work with a will. The beads on his abacus flew back and forth as he totted up the cost. He asked for clarification on the number of swivels as they had asked for a lot. He also raised his eyebrows at the number of Nock volley guns.

"If I didn't know better, I would say you were preparing this ship for chasing and boarding as well as giving someone a nasty surprise if they tried boarding you." He observed as he added in the cost of five-hundred grenades.

"To save time and because I know you," he said as he finished and wrote down the final sum. "I will cut straight to the drop-dead price. Two thousand three hundred and fifty-nine pounds."

Tom looked at Marty and they exchanged the slightest of nods.

"When can it all be delivered?" he asked.

"Fastest I can gather this lot together will be at least a month and then I need to move it up river to St. Catherine's Dock. That will take a couple of days by barge." Fletcher replied.

"That's a deal then." Marty said opened the saddleback and emptied it on Fletcher's desk. "That's twelve hundred on account in gold."

Fletcher roared with laughter. "I knew you would know how much! My offer still stands my friend. Anytime you want to go into business just call me."

Chapter 20 Manning and Arming Up

"I think he likes you," Tom observed as the mounted up and rode back towards London. "but how does he know so much about the ship an' all."

"Fletcher has fingers in many pies, just like my dear wife, and just like my wife likes to think he is cleverer than the rest of us. I saw one of his men hanging around the dock two days ago."

"Does he keep an eye on you in particular?" Tom asked obviously concerned

"No, I think he was watching the ship, sensing a business opportunity probably." Marty reassured him.

They got back to London in good time even though it started to snow. The horses were happy to get back to their stables in the muse and the two men stamped their way into the house through the back door. Marty froze as he heard shouting. He pulled out his barkers from his coat pockets checked the priming was dry and moved forward. He heard a double click from behind and to his left and knew Tom had his back.

There was a crash and Marty resisted the temptation to run. He continued moving forward deliberately. They got to the hallway and the front door was open, the lock broken. The noise was coming from the drawing room. He moved up to the door taking position on the side with the handle and Tom positioned himself to the hinge side.

He reached out turned the knob and pushed the door off the latch, counted down from three to one, shoved it open, took a step through and dropped to a knee. Tom was stood behind him and had a clear field of fire over Marty's head. Caroline was in the opposite corner holding a vase, ready to throw it at two ruffians who had their backs to Marty and

Tom. She was screaming and cursing like a fish wife so the two never heard the door open.

Marty put his pistols on the floor and drew his knife, he stepped up to the first of the men and hit him hard on the back of the head with the hilt. Then he kicked out to the side hitting the other man in the side of the left knee wrecking it. As he collapsed, he stepped in stamped out with his boot hitting him in the side of the head.

There was a shout from outside and then Blaez came through the door teeth bared and proceeded to savage the one Marty had clubbed. Marty gentled him and then went and took Caroline in his arms.

"They waited till Hanson (the butler) took Blaez out for a walk, then broke the lock on the door and came in demanding my jewels." Caroline sobbed. She looked down at one her now prone assailants, stepped away from Marty and kicked one three or four times in the ribs.

Marty looked at the broken crockery on the floor and identified a couple of really expensive vases. He couldn't help wondering if it would have been cheaper to give then a couple of rings.

Someone had gone out and fetched a Bow Street Runner and the constable turned up, took one look at the two, now semi-conscious, but groggy, men and said.

"Tim Standing and Peter Butcher, both known to us. The judge warned them Newgate wouldn't be their destination next time they got caught. This time they will hang." Marty had no sympathy, both men were obviously habitual criminals and knew the risk they were taking.

The next morning Tom went out and found a carpenter who would build them a new door at short notice and a locksmith that could fit a reliable lock. In the meantime, he and Marty fixed large deadbolts to keep the door closed. Another constable came and took detailed statements, which they signed, and informed them they didn't need to attend the court which would be held the next morning. Justice would be quick and final.

Marty turned his attention to the security of the house. There were only two men on the staff, the butler and a coachman the rest were all women including the two servants that had come back from India with them. One of which was now walking out with Tom. He contacted an agency and asked them to send him candidates for a pair of footmen. He specified ex-military men who were married.

Five were sent and Marty selected three to be interviewed by Caroline. Two were ex-Army and the third ex-Navy, all three could look after themselves and handle weapons. The interviews complete, Caroline expressed a preference for the Navy man and the older of the two Army men. Frederick Cooper and Arthur Standish plus wives joined the Stockley household.

Marty took both men shopping, man style. He took them to a gunsmith and had them select pistols for themselves. Then he visited a backstreet shop that he knew and bought blackjacks and short clubs. Last they visited his tailor and had them measured for the house livery with special pockets for the pistols and a long pocket in the trousers for the clubs.

All that done he was able to turn his attention back to The Tempest. He had two complete sets of sails being made and once the Larks and Marines arrived, they would start replacing the old worn rigging, but first he knew she needed her bottom cleaned and inspected. She probably needed new copper and her deck needed strengthening to take the bigger guns.

He negotiated with a commercial shipyard on the Thames to put her into drydock and, luckily, that time of year they had several empty bays and were grateful for the work. They had her towed over to the yard and into the dock at high tide. A set of lock gates were closed across the entrance and as the tide ran out the water in the dock was allowed to run away through a sluice. The Sluice was then closed leaving the ship high and dry on wooden stocks.

The weed and barnacles were scraped and burnt off and she was inspected. For a ship of her age she wasn't in too bad condition. A couple of copper sheets had thinned and had holes in, and there were a couple of soft planks that needed to be replaced, but all in all she was in good shape. Marty dug into his own pocket and had all the copper replaced as the budget given to the S.O.F. wouldn't stretch to that. He considered that a good investment, and he would get his money back with interest.

By luck the Larks arrived while she was in dock and got to work replacing the rigging and any blocks that were worn out. Marty, Tom and Wilson went out recruiting. The Navy would man the tempest with one hundred and fifty men and officers but as a privateer Marty wanted at least two hundred or even two hundred and fifty eventually, but for now, he would settle for one hundred and fifty and look for the rest when he got to the other side of the Atlantic.

He had sixty men from the Lark and S.O.F and was letting it be known that they were recruiting for a 'private' venture. Marty wanted seasoned hands, he didn't care what country they came from or what their background outside of sailing was.

After she was back in the water, they opened the recruitment proper and a steady stream of men started to show up at the gangplank. James and Tom set up a desk on the dock and interviewed them. Tom played his part well, he was acting as the first mate because of his age and James as second mate. James took the inversion in their ranks in his stride, he had always respected Tom as Marty's Cox.

The applicants ranged from experienced seamen, some who had probably run from the Navy, to the desperate who just wanted to try and escape their wretched lives.

Marty soon realised they needed a surgeon or physician to check the health of the potential new recruits, so he went to talk to their family doctor. He didn't say much when Marty told him he was looking for someone for a long sea voyage, just wrote a name and an address on a paper and handed it to him. He had a sad look about him when he did it which puzzled Marty.

The address was a town house in a muse that was reasonably well to do. Marty knocked at the door and it was opened by a maid who ushered him in when he asked to see Mr Shelby. He was shown into what, was obviously, a consulting room, so he sat and waited. Ten minutes later Shelby walked in, he was around thirty years old with brown hair tending to grey, a sallow complexion, piercing blue eyes that had a haunted look and was as thin as a rake.

"What can I do for you Mr ...?" He asked looking Marty up and down.

"Martin Stanwell, I was given your name by a mutual friend."

"Were you." he said flatly. "Sent here to help me no doubt."

"Not to help you, but to offer you a position and the chance to escape this dreary town for sunnier climes," Marty replied.

Shelby looked at him quizzically.

"And who sent you to me to offer that?" he asked.

"He asked that he remains incognito, but he was very sure you would be interested."

"Well you have my attention. What is your offer?"

"I am setting up an expedition to the Caribbean and my ship is in need of a physician, someone who know about the fevers and diseases of the Islands and who can do more than just chop off limbs. Someone who can keep my crew healthy," Marty explained.

"There will be combat?" Shelby asked.

"Probably," Marty replied.

Shelby started to walk up and down muttering softly to himself.

"When do you need me to start?" he asked.

"Well if you aren't doing anything urgent, I would say straight away, I am recruiting my crew and want to have them checked out."

Shelby stopped pacing and looked Marty in the eyes.

"You don't want to know why I would accept such a post?"

"Frankly I don't care as long as you are sober, care for my men and are professional." Marty stated emphatically. "I don't want to lose them to disease or wounds unnecessarily."

"One last question. Why is Lord Candor working under a nom de plume and setting up a privateer, when he is known to be in the Navy."

Marty grinned at him.

"When we are at sea and away from prying eyes and ears, I will tell you, but I will want your oath now that you will not share that observation with anyone. Even if you don't take the post."

Shelby looked at the earnest young man sat in front of him and sensed his passion, what he had heard Nelson call zeal.

"You have my word on that," he held his hand up to forestall any comment from Marty. "I have my own reasons for joining, which, for now, will remain my own and your mission, whatever it is, intrigues me. Now my fee?"

"You will get a retainer of twenty guineas a year, plus you can charge the crew for special treatments such as the clap and you get a share of any prize money. I will pay to stock your drugs cabinet and for any special instruments or tools you need." Marty explained.

Shelby took a deep breath and let it out slowly and then held out his hand.

"My thanks to whoever gave you my name and I accept the position. Where can I join your ship?"

Marty returned to The Tempest and reviewed his list of officers and warrants. He had Tom as First Mate, James as Second, Shelby as surgeon. He wasn't sure what position to give Paul as they officially didn't have marines onboard, but Master at Arms sounded good. The marine, Sheldon, who had admitted to having been a clerk in a former life was made 'purser' to help Marty with provisioning. John Smith stayed as Quartermaster. Wilson was made Bosun. He needed a carpenter, sailmaker and a sailing master.

He got a surprise when Harbrook from the Tool Shed turned up and gave him a box of timers.

"The boss said you could use these," he told Marty as he handed them over. He looked around the ship and asked.

"Is yer going privateering?"

Marty thanked him then replied.

"Yes, we are going pirate hunting as well."

"You will want to be boarding ships then, well me and the boys have been thinking about that and how we have to get real close to chuck the grapnels across," he stated. "We have come up with an idea of how to fire them out of swivels. That way you can fire them across into t'other ship's rigging at pistol shot range."

Marty thought about that. When they boarded another ship they traditionally came right up alongside, and men threw the grapnels to tie the two ships together. There was usually a high casualty rate amongst those men as they were targeted by any sharpshooters on the other ship. If this idea worked then it would help protect the men and cut down casualties. The down side was they would be further from the other ship with more chance he might turn away. On balance he decided it would be more of a benefit than a hazard.

"When can you get me some of those?" He asked.

Harbrook grinned and said.

"No time at all. I got fifty grapnels in the cart on the dock."

Marty called Paul and went down to the dock to check out the invention. Whereas the traditional grapnel had an eye on the end of the shaft for attaching a line, these beasts had the eye attached where the four hooks joined together at the top of the shaft. The shaft itself was about two foot six long and had a wooden plug the diameter of a swivel bore rammed on the end and another two thirds of the way up.

"You put a half charge in the swivel, then a wad, then slide the hook in so it's all the way in to here." He pointed to a notch filed into the shaft about three inches below the hooks. "You have the line coiled nicely to the side, so it runs free when you shoot the hook at the other ship."

"Brilliant idea!" Paul said admiringly.

"An' don't forget to tie off the bitter end," Harbrook added as a final thought preening slightly at the praise.

Marty gave him three guineas, one for each of the Tool Shed team as a personal reward for their initiative.

His next stop was to a pub near to the India dock. He made conversation with the landlord and let him know he was looking for a sailing master, carpenter and sailmaker as well as prime hands. For a sovereign he promised to let Marty know if any ships were being paid off.

Next, he visited the sailmaker where he was having his sails made. The shed was huge, and the floor was covered in acres of pristine white canvas apart from one area where there was a small sea of red. Marty walked over to it and was joined by the owner.

"These will put the fear of God into anyone who sees them," he observed.

Marty nodded.

"That is the idea. Better they give up without a fight than we have to force the issue."

"Privateering must be mighty profitable then. Canvas that colour, that won't fade too fast, is twice the price of white," he observed.

"When will they be ready along with the standard white set?" Marty asked.

"Well, we are on time so far and haven't had any major setbacks, so the end of January still looks good."

Marty thanked him and went back to the ship.

Shelby the physician had arrived and was checking over the recruits. He was far more thorough than a Navy surgeon would have been. He had a book into which he entered each man's name, then added a brief description of his background and his physical condition. Marty looked over his shoulder as he wrote and saw there was a third entry where he designated them fit or unfit for the rating they were applying for. Occasionally he would mark someone as fit but who needed extra food or had a curable affliction.

He had also signed as fit a number of ship's boys, unusual for a privateer, but Tom had pointed out that they did many jobs the men would sniff at and it also gave a home to many poor waifs that would struggle to survive in the city.

Satisfied all was going well and considering it was coming up to Christmas he made his farewells to the boys and made his way home.

Caroline had decided that she would spend Christmas in London and had sent instructions to the Cheshire estate to prepare the usual celebration in their absence for the tenants and estate workers. In London the house was decorated with pine, holly and mistletoe. The two new footmen were especially useful in this as they were both easily the tallest members of the household and could reach to pin the boughs in place around the door frames.

Two large geese were hanging in the larder along with a selection of gamebirds. The cook was planning a five-bird roast. She would debone goose, capon, duck, pheasant and woodcock then place the birds in order of size on top of each other. She would then add a forcemeat stuffing and reform the goose by stitching up the breast with everything else inside. She made two, one for the house and the other at Marty's request to be sent down the Tempest for the crew that was already on board. He would also send down a couple of casks of good beer and a keg of rum. The ship's cook would prepare potatoes, vegetables and the plumb duff onboard.

James and Paul visited them for Christmas along with Admiral Hood and his wife Susannah. Armand was invited but had already agreed to spend the feast day with his in-laws, but the numbers were more than made up by Caroline's sister Julia, her husband, Captain Cockburn, and their four teenage children.

The happy day arrived, and they all attended a service at Grosvenor Chapel, it was expected and if they didn't it would be noted. Dinner was set for three o'clock in the afternoon and was a veritable feast. Not only was there the five-bird roast but a rib of beef, a joint of pork with beautifully crispy skin, and a whole ham that had been studded with cloves and boiled in cider. Roast and boiled potatoes, winter kale, honey baked parsnips, buttered carrots, brussels sprouts, mashed swede with lashings of butter and nutmeg, and a rich gravy made from the giblets of the fowl. For dessert there were a selection of Possets, plumb duff and custard, jellies, fruit and nuts. A selection of cheeses was laid out on a board in case anyone had room left.

The wine flowed! Bottles of Rhenish white and champagne as an aperitif followed by rich Burgundy and Bordeaux reds with the main course. The desert was washed down with sweet Madeira and port.

After they had eaten to bursting the men retired to the library where Marty had had a new billiards table installed. The older of Cockburn's boys joined them being fourteen and sixteen respectively and midshipmen in their own right.

While the men played and drank brandy the ladies sat in the drawing room chatting and the children played quietly with their new toys with Blaez watching them intently. Caroline went to a drawer in the dresser and took out a packet of folded tissue paper. She carefully unfolded it and spilled a half a dozen sapphires and rubies into Julia's hand.

"They are beautiful!" she exclaimed. "Are they from India?"

"The sapphires are from Ceylon the Rubies are from India." Caroline replied. "I want you to have them as my Christmas present to you."

"But," Julia started to object.

"But nothing." Caroline interrupted. "If it wasn't for you in the time I was married to Wilfred, I would have gone mad. Now I have a chance to do something nice for you."

"Oh Caroline! Just seeing you so happy with Martin is enough," she looked at the sparkling gems in her hand. "but thank you, they are truly wonderful."

"Get them made into something you will wear often to remind you of me." Caroline said and hugged her.

Boxing day Marty and Caroline were left to themselves in the house. All the servants had been loaded up with the leftover food from the feast the day before and went home to their families. What was left after that was picked up by the local vicar and his wife to be distributed to the poor. Marty hated waste and had a conscience due to his background.

They took a cab to the dock and visited The Tempest. Marty dressed as his alter ego and Caroline chose a simple dress that could have been worn by any woman with a moderately wealthy husband. Blaez tagged along, he needed the exercise as the children had slipped him a huge quantity of titbits during dinner the day before.

Marty was half expecting the ship to be a drunken mess but to his surprise the ship was disciplined and relatively sober. He heard a voice say "Be that is missus? Blimey I would stay at home for ever if she were mine!" Which made him smile and also wonder why he wandered. Caroline won the hearts of every man she met. She emphasised her native Sheffield accent and flirted outrageously, playing the pirate's doxy for all it was worth but retaining a certain level of class at the same time.

There were about ninety men onboard and another thirty due to join in the new year. Tom thought that word of the Christmas feast would get around and men would think that Marty was a generous captain and want to be on his crew, and he shouldn't worry they would have a full crew when they sailed.

Marty had paid a visit to a talented wood carver by the name of John Seaton and commissioned a new figurehead which he had mounted while they were there. It was a demonic looking bust depicting a male head with wild hair, pursed lips and puffed cheeks like it was blowing a gale. When it was mounted it did, he thought, look quite savage. The men loved it.

At the end of January, a pair of barges pulled into the dock and Fletcher delivered the cannon and other weapons that Marty had ordered. The powder was waiting at a secluded dock further down river as the city, understandably, didn't approve of explosives being loaded in the port of London.

They were almost there, as by then, they had one hundred and forty-two crew signed on and were in the luxury position of being able to cherry pick the last few. Marty planned to sail in the first week of March after his birthday. He would be twenty-three years old.

He called a meeting of the officers.

"We will sail on the second of March. The ship needs to be provisioned for three months. If we get lucky and we make a fast crossing, we should be at English Harbour to recruit our extra hands and re-provision by mid-April. The new water casks are the only thing we are waiting for and will be here next week so I think we can make that comfortably. We will warp out of here and down to the dock to load our powder in two weeks, once that's aboard I want us to sail down the Thames and make a shakedown cruise to settle the crew in." He looked at Shelby and James. "Where are we now with the crew?"

"We have a full complement of topmen, the landlord of that pub down by India dock sent a message that an Indiaman was decommissioning, and we managed to pick up most of her crew before they were snapped up by anyone else. We could still do with a dozen more landsmen, especially some for the afterguard." James reported.

"The health of the recruits is generally good, especially those who are experienced sailors. I had to reject a number who had hernias or were pox ridden. There are a number who are generally healthy but underfed, those I have onboard on special diets to build them up." Shelby informed them.

Marty was surprised and somewhat gratified by that and was quietly very pleased he had found Shelby, who continued, "I have ensured that we will have an ample supply of lemon and lime juice onboard and insist that all the men get a portion of one or the other with their rum ration. This will prevent scurvy and reduce other common complaints."

He looked at the Purser who nodded then at Marty and asked. "I see that you are feeding the men lots of fresh vegetables while we are in port. How long does that continue once we are at sea?"

"We generally run out of fresh food after three weeks. The larger livestock will all have been eaten by then so the crew will be fed salt beef and pork with dried peas and ships biscuit. The officers will eat whatever they have in their personal stores until they run out and then be eating the same food as the men. We will restock with fresh vegetables, fruit, water and livestock every time we enter port if we can," Marty explained.

Shelby nodded and made some notes in his ever-present notebook.

At the end of the meeting Marty was presented with inventories and lists of all the stores that had been delivered so far and he settled down with the Purser to enter it all into the ship's books.

Chapter 21: Shake down

Two weeks later, with a complement of one hundred and seventy-five, they warped out of the dock and on to the Thames proper. The time came to make their way down stream on the ebb tide and with a light Southwest breeze they set sail. Marty was thankful that the master, Arnold Greys, they had picked up from the Indiaman was experienced in navigating the river, because it frankly terrified him. There were mudbanks aplenty to trap the unwary and the Thames barges were not often inclined to give way to a private ship. The river was as twisty as a snake in heat and the crew were kept busy setting the sails over and over again.

They made the dock where they would load their powder. Fletcher was waiting for them and came aboard as soon as they docked and asked to speak to Marty in private.

"What can I do for you Mr Fletcher," Marty asked as they settled down over a glass of Madeira.

"I have to ask a favour of you Martin, if I may," Fletcher replied. "I find that I need to, shall we say, absent myself from these shores for a while due to a certain misunderstanding with some, ahh, gentlemen who I have done some business with." He looked uncomfortable and embarrassed as he said it and somewhat desperate.

"A deal gone wrong?" Marty asked and held up his hand to forestall any answer. "No matter I don't need or want to know, but luckily for you I need a man who can value goods and help negotiate a good price on their disposal, keep track of the ship's provisions and keep the books. I think that would suit you well." He smiled his wolf smile.

Fletcher knew when he was in no position to negotiate, the 'gentlemen' he had upset were quite capable of ending his life and he was not yet ready to leave this mortal coil.

"Agreed. Anything else?"

Marty laughed and said.

"No, I won't take advantage of you as you dealt fairly with me. You will be a member of the crew this way not a passenger and if there is prize money will get a share of it."

That made all the difference to Fletcher as he had expected to have to pay his way. He knew that Marty was doing him a favour and he wouldn't forget it. He held out his hand and said.

"Thank you, Martin. My name is Jonathan by the way."

Marty shook it and said, "You call me skipper in front of the men, Tom is my number two and you will take orders from him and James whenever they are on watch. You will have a separate cabin on the Orlop deck and not be expected to take part in the sailing of the ship. If we get into a fight, you can help the surgeon or stay in your cabin as you wish. If you have baggage to bring aboard tell Tom and he will get it on as soon as the powder is loaded."

Fletcher thanked him again and left the cabin. '*Well that was unexpected,*' Marty thought '*but probably a blessing in disguise. At least I won't have to do the damn books myself now.*' With that he went up on deck whistling a merry shanty.

The loading of the powder was completed, and they set sail for the run out of the Wash. They sailed due East to get out into the middle of the Channel and then turned Southwest to take them through the gap between Dover and Calais. He wanted to get them out onto open water before he started pushing the boat and its crew. There was just too much traffic to be playing.

A turn to the west took them along the South coast of England. He resisted the temptation to call in at Poole but instead made for the Lizard. There he would take them out into the Atlantic where he would have the sea room he required.

The weather was, to say the least, brisk with a moderately strong wind and rolling waves coming from the west. He ordered a series of sail evolutions and had them repeated them until he was happy. Then he started them on bringing down the top masts and yards and sending them back up again.

In between he exercised the guns. He had a gunner who claimed to be experienced but after a disastrous exercise, where it was apparent that none of the cartridge that were brought up from the magazine were the same size, that was sent into doubt. He had him brought in front of him and examined his knowledge in an extensive interview. To say the least, the man was found wanting and was immediately relegated to the landsmen, to be put ashore at the earliest opportunity.

He now had a problem; he needed a good gunner and they were as rare as hen's teeth. John Smith stood in and did a better job than the former incumbent but that was not a long-term solution as he wanted John as Quartermaster.

Marty decided he would call in at Falmouth and see if he could find anyone there. They dropped anchor in the bay and Marty and James went ashore. They wandered into the town and picked a pub which looked like it was frequented by salts. Marty had a word with the landlord and then stood in front of the fireplace.

"Ahoy there!" he bellowed above the noise of laughter and chatter, and once it died down, he announced.

"I have need of a gunner for my 'private' ship The Tempest. We are bound for the Caribbean under a letter of marque. If you are qualified or you know anyone who is then let me know. There is money in it for the man who gets me the right man." He flipped a golden guinea in the air at that point then walked back to the bar and picked up his tankard of ale.

After around twenty minutes there was a tap on his shoulder. He turned around ready to defend himself but found himself face to face with one of the ugliest men he had ever seen. He was short and had a misshapen face to the extent that one eye was slightly higher than the other and his head looked as if it was somehow twisted. He had huge shoulders, long arms, out of proportion to his body, short legs and a hint of a hump on his back.

"I am a qualified gunner," he said in a surprisingly refined voice. "My friend here has told me you are looking for one," There was a man stood behind him who was watching and listening anxiously, "but if I go, he comes with me."

Marty looked from one to the other and understood, but as long as it stayed between them, he didn't give a damn.

"We can accommodate that," Marty said. "but first let's see if you really do have what I want.,

He led them over to an empty table and proceeded to interview the man thoroughly. It turns out his name was Ian Wolverton and he was the son of a squire. His father had all but rejected him because of his deformities but his mother made sure he had an education and he joined the Navy as a teenager. He discovered a love for gunnery and proved himself worthy of being rated gunner, but with the peace he was put ashore when his ship was decommissioned, and no further places were offered.

He knew his gunnery and answered all Marty's questions easily and with confidence. His companion, Jonathan Moore didn't say anything until Marty asked him what his rating was.

"Gunner's Mate." *'Appropriate that,'* Marty thought.

The two of them met them at the dock in the morning and Marty signalled for his boat to come over and pick them up. Wolverton was agile despite his deformities and entered the boat without any assistance from Moore. When he boarded, he went up the side easily and when he got to the deck stood glaring at the crew daring them to make a comment.

"Be that you Ian?" came a lone voice and one of the Bosun's Mates stepped forward. "Well I'm damned if it aint!" The two men clasped forearms and slapped each other on the shoulder.

The Mate looked around the deck and said in a loud voice.

"This be my mate Gunner Wolverton. We sailed together on the old Bedford and he be a damn fine Gunner and saw action with me at the Saints," and that was that.

They anchored in The Downs. Marty didn't want to do anything that could associate the S.O.F. with The Tempest and James and Tom had suggested they lay up there as it was least conspicuous. He was surprised when The Lark approached them and tied up on their starboard side. A look over the side revealed that Armand, Susie and their baby were on board with a smiling Caroline, Beth and James. He immediately ordered a sling rigged and turned to see a grinning Tom already swinging a bosun's chair over the side. He had the feeling he had been set up.

Several packages were slung on board as well as enough beer for the crew to have a wet. Marty was puzzled then realised it was the twenty eighth of February, his birthday! Roland du Demaine was another passenger and he headed straight for the kitchens once he had greeted Marty French style with a kiss on both cheeks.

Down in his cabin Armand informed him the Roland would be staying as his birthday gift to him. He had heard that their cook was more of the Navy breed, more suited to catering for the crew than a captain and Roland was volunteered. Roland didn't mind at all he was bored with life at the farm, especially as Armand mostly ate with his family these days.

Soon delicious smells were emanating from the galley, the beer kegs were broached, and the crew filed past to get a tankard full. Down in his cabin a party was started. Blaez was keeping the children occupied playing tug and keeping young Beth from wandering off. The adults drank and ate the wonderful meal Roland prepared. They had fresh mussels cooked in wine and garlic, followed by venison, that Roland had slow cooked in red wine back at the farm and finished in the galley. That was followed by a creation Rolland called Crème Brûlée which was a baked custard with sugar burnt on top by a hot iron, so it had melted and gone crisp.

After they had finished eating, and the men were passing the port, Beth came to Marty and held out a neatly wrapped package to him. She was very serious and said "Wappy birday daddy" and when he took it grinned from ear to ear. He carefully opened it and inside, in a silver gilt frame was perfect portrait of his children. When she saw the smile on his face Beth crowed in delight and jumped up and down in a little dance that made him grab her and cover her face in kisses, which just made her giggle all the more. He also gathered up young James and was about to do the same for him when he saw his face was covered in jelly and cream. He settled for a hug and gave him back to Blaez to look after.

Once he had thanked the children properly, Caroline handed him a present from her. It was a much smaller box and he opened it very carefully. Inside nestled on a bed of silk was a beautiful, gold, double hunter pocket watch and chain made by Breguet. Not only was it beautiful but Breguet's watches were the most accurate of the time and would aid him in his navigation. Inside the rear case was an inscription.

From loves first kiss
You were my hero

Caroline

There was a button hole bar in the middle of the chain and on the other end to the watch was a locket with, in one side a miniature of her and a lock of her hair under glass in the other.

Marty took her in his arms and kissed her and when they disentangled, to cheers from the rest of the party, she put the watch in his right waistcoat pocket, the locket in the left and hooked the bar through a buttonhole at the appropriate height.

Chapter 22: First Blood

The next morning as the tide turned, The Tempest made her way out to sea and headed west to be able to make a southing to clear Ushant. She sailed well, Marty thought as they passed The Needles and the Isle of Wight. He wanted to get up to around Falmouth and preferable Penzance, before they turned south.

They made the turn the next day at around eleven o'clock and had a fair wind. Marty had them run through several sail evolutions for an hour and then practice with the guns. At one o'clock they stopped for the crew to have their midday meal. Roland was not only cooking for him but was supervising the cook for the men's meals, which ultimately meant the food was tastier and more nutritious than the standard fare.

He ran more sail evolutions in the afternoon and was pleased that the men were starting to work more as a team. The evolutions were beginning to run smoother and with less confusion, there were no injuries to speak of, so he invited Shelby to dine with him that evening along with James.

After the first course of a fine fish soup, Roland had lines run from the stern and had ship's boys manning them to trawl for fish, they settled down to a dish of beef in a wine sauce with small onions in it. Shelby looked up from his plate and asked.

"Well we are certainly out to sea now so will you tell me why we are here Milord?"

"One thing first, please don't call me that again, even in private." Marty cautioned him.

Shelby nodded and muttered an apology.

"The British holdings in the Caribbean have reported an upsurge in piracy from French and American 'privateers' and have reported that they believe that the Spanish may also be joining in."

"Aren't we supposed to be at peace with them?" asked Shelby.

"Technically yes, but they have a rich tradition of piracy so if any of their ships are involved, they will not be carrying letters of marque."

"Which makes them fair game." James observed with a feral grin.

"Absolutely. Now the Royal Navy is spread very thin over there and cannot hope to be able to escort every convoy, let alone single traders making it easy pickings for the pirates." Marty continued. "We are going to get in amongst them, find out where their bases are and eliminate as many as we can." Marty continued.

"Are you part of the Navy?" Shelby asked.

"Yes, but that is all I can tell you for now." Marty explained.

Shelby thought about that for a minute or two.

"Answer me one question then," he asked. "If you are Royal Navy, why do you need a letter of marque?"

Marty looked at him steadily for an uncomfortably long time.

"I want you word of honour that anything I tell you from this point on will never be repeated to anyone."

Shelby looked a little startled but then gave his word. Marty then explained their role and involvement with the Intelligence Service and their mission.

"Now I fully understand if you object to being involved on the grounds of honour or whatever and will put you on the first ship bound for England that we meet." Marty concluded still giving him the same flat stare.

"Oh, my no! I mean certainly not! No don't do that!" Shelby spluttered. "This is just what I need, and this trip will further my studies into tropical diseases."

Marty looked at him quizzically.

Shelby sighed and explained.

"I was married to my childhood sweetheart, but I got so tied up in my studies that I neglected her. We were never wealthy, because I spent more time researching than practicing professional medicine, so she couldn't even circulate with the ladies of her own class as she was ashamed of her wardrobe and appearance. In the end she met another man, fell in love and left me. I was, and still am, devastated by that and must admit that I immersed myself in my studies to an even greater extent. My friends tried to lift me out of it but I wasn't interested and so they too started to leave me in my misery. Only two stayed in touch, one of whom, probably, introduced me for this position knowing that I would be attracted to the chance to study in the tropics first hand.

I have now rediscovered my love of medicine in general and am fascinated by the challenge life aboard a ship presents. The mission is intriguing, and I must confess somewhat exciting."

Marty grinned at him and raised a glass.

"Then I propose a toast. To excitement, discovery and rejuvenation!"

They drained their glasses to heeltaps and banged them on the table for refills.

Marty awoke before dawn as usual and took the time just to lay in his cot and feel the way the ship was handling. He could hear the watch coming up on deck and before they were called to quarters (even though they weren't Navy he did that as a precaution) he got up and dressed. He climbed up on the quarterdeck and quietly checked the log and the compass. If he was right, they should be around half way across the Bay of Biscay. The weather was fair, and he could see high scudding clouds just showing in the pre-dawn light passing from the West.

He watched as the horizon turned first grey, then started to brighten and was surprised when the lookout called.

"Sail Ho! Fine on the Larboard Quarter! About a mile away!"

He grabbed a telescope and climbed up on to a carronade, steadying himself on a stay.

He spotted it almost immediately. A brig flying the French flag.

"Three points to Larboard! Load the Larboard guns, chain shot!" He cried.

He leapt back onto the quarterdeck and was met by James who had left his cot and rushed on deck to see what was afoot.

"French brig, looks like a merchantman but I'm not sure about that." Marty told him. "He hasn't seen us; we are still in the shadow."

Marty was right the sun hadn't risen enough yet to show them and he thought that they could close to within half a mile before they were spotted if they were lucky.

"Carronades load with cannister over ball and target his quarterdeck then rigging once we are within two cables."

'Time to show them and the crew our new colours,' Marty thought with a smile. He had secretly had a new flag made and now sent James down to his cabin with instructions to fetch it from where he had left it. James was back in minutes with the package.

"Raise it on the mizzen," Marty instructed.

The flag soared up the lanyard. It was black and emblazoned on it in white was a fighting knife depicted point down through a skull over a pair of crossed pistols. As it unfurled a cheer went up from the men and they shook their weapons or gun tools in the air.

Tom appeared and he was carrying Marty's fighting harness and a silk shirt. Marty changed into the shirt and Tom helped him into the harness. When Marty was set, he held out his double-barrelled pistols.

"Loaded and primed," he growled as he handed them over.

Blaez jumped up from the deck and came to stand by Marty. He had his spiked collar on and looked fierce. Marty patted him on the head and thanked Tom for both of them.

Marty checked the range and saw that there was some frantic activity on the deck of the brig.

"Take in the mains! Topsails and royals only." Marty commanded in preparation to engage.

John Smith had taken over the wheel and Tom was down commanding the main guns. He had the quoins almost all the way out to send their chain into the brigs rigging.

"Bring her up beam to beam John," he barked over his shoulder.

The Tempest swung so she was sailing on a slightly converging course with the brig at around four cables so she could bring her main guns to bear. Marty looked at Tom and nodded.

"By Broadside," he bellowed and then paused waiting for the ship to start the up roll, "FIRE!"

The twelve-pound guns went off almost together, the chain howled across the gap and thrashed through the brigs rigging. The effect was satisfying as stays were cut and the main yard was sent crashing to the deck, but the brig wasn't finished, and her gun ports swung open. Marty watched with almost detached interest as her guns were run out. He counted nine nine-pounders which spouted fingers of flame, followed by a cloud of smoke.

Tom had his crews reloading when the French shot howled through the rigging. A couple of blocks fell, one barely missing one of the ship's boys. The marines in the tops got away without injury as the French had fired a little early on the roll and their shot went through at around main yard height.

John had closed the gap while the guns were being reloaded and as soon as he saw they were ready, swung the wheel for them to fire. The second broadside was even more devastating than the first. The brig's foremast took a direct hit above the futtock shrouds and snapped off, falling over their larboard side. The sails on the main were both shredded.

The French guns ran out again. *That was fast.* Marty thought. *Too fast for a merchant.* The muzzles blossomed with fire and part of the transom disappeared in a shower of splinters leaving several men lying on the deck wounded.

They were now two cable apart.

"Carronades!" Marty ordered.

CHUFF-BOOM they spoke almost simultaneously. Marty was pleased that the gun captains had obviously agreed that the forward one would target the Mizzen mast and the aft the quarterdeck.

'Oh, that's nice,' Marty thought as the smoke cleared and he could see that the quarterdeck was no longer manned, and the mizzen was wobbling.

Tom had reloaded the twelves with grape and as John closed the gap to a cable let go the broadside straight at their gun ports.

CHUFF-BOOM the carronades spoke again and this time they both aimed to sweep the deck.

At near pistol shot, there was a ripple of fire from the swivels mounted along the rail and grapnels sailed across to put the brig in a death grip. Paul La Pierre was marshalling the boarders.

The ships ground together, and Marty called.

"BOARDERS AWAY!"

"YEAH, YEAH, YEAH, YEAH, YEEEEHHHAAAAA!" came the battle cry from the former Larks as they swarmed over the side onto the French deck.

Marty was almost the first over, had his sword in his right and a pistol in his left. A screaming French sailor launched himself at him swinging a cutlass in a huge roundhouse blow which Marty ducked under while skewering him through the abdomen with his sword.

A second later a boarding pike passed about an inch in front of his nose from his right, followed by a scream. A glance showed him that Blaez had his jaws clamped on the unfortunate man's arm. Marty ignored him as he was no longer a threat but turned his attention to a new assailant coming in from his left.

This one looked more dangerous as he was advancing in a controlled way and looked as if he knew how to use the, what looked like, a three-quarter length rapier. A gentleman's weapon.

Marty turned to face him cocking his pistol against his forearm. He raised it, pointing straight at the man's face.

"*Yield.*" he said in French.

The man stopped dead and after looking into Marty's eyes lowered his weapon and stepped back. Marty turned away as he saw a movement at the edge of his vision and parried a blow from a marlin spike that was aimed at his head. He shot the man at point blank range though the centre of his chest.

A warning shouted in his mind and he spun back to the 'gentleman' just in time to knock a thrust from his sword aside with his pistol barrel. They faced off.

Marty dropped the pistol and drew his knife, dropping into a fighting stance.

His opponent feigned an attack in low, which Marty parried with his hanger, and then followed up with a main gauche that he had hidden behind his back.

Marty blocked with his knife and disengaged.

The circled counter clockwise. Marty wasn't aware but the fight was over around most of the ship and the men from both sides were watching.

He stepped in and attacked high, swinging for the eyes.

His opponent parried, letting Marty's blade slide up and over his head and instead of backing away, stepped forward to attack with his left.

Marty caught the blade with his knife and the two men ended up face to face, their swords locked above their heads and their knives locked between their chests.

Marty grinned and headbutted him on the bridge of the nose.

His opponent staggered back, stunned by the unexpected blow.

Marty stepped in to run him through the heart with his hanger, but a blind swing slapped his blade away.

The main gauche slashed around keeping him at bay.

Blinking his eyes free of tears, his opponent resumed the on-guard position. Blood ran from his nose which was obviously broken. *'That has got to hurt.'*

Marty defended a two-handed series of attacks as his opponent tried to finish the fight. It ended when he stepped on an eyebolt and momentarily lost his balance.

Marty thrust with his sword piercing his neck, cutting the carotid artery sending a spray of blood across the deck. He followed up with slash of his knife that all but decapitated the man.

There were cheers from The Tempests and groans from the French.

The brig was theirs. The man Marty had fought was the Captain who hadn't been on the quarterdeck when the carronades had spun their deadly load.

She was the Faisan and was a country ship dressed up to look like a merchantman to trap unwary British ships. They stripped her of everything of value or that might be useful then sailed her down to Gibraltar.

Shelby went over and treated the wounded that could be saved, and they dispatched the ones without hope. Of The

Tempests, several had splinters removed and others had cuts stitched. There were no amputations. Marty noted that Shelby cleaned his instruments with brandy, which was flamed off, before every operation.

Once they moored up in the harbour Marty went ashore with Blaez, Tom and Fletcher to find an agent to sell the brig. They called in at Coutts to open an account in his assumed name and enquired after an agent. They were directed to a man called Eldritch who ran a shipyard.

"Good afternoon gentlemen, what can I do for you?" greeted Eldritch as they entered his office.

"We have a prize we want to dispose of, and we were given your name as someone who could help." Marty said shaking the man's hand.

"She's a French built brig, slightly damaged but nothing that a man like you couldn't put right in a moment."

"You mean the one moored over by that Jackass Frigate over yonder?" Eldritch asked nodding in the general direction of their mooring.

"That's the one." Tom answered.

"If I sell her for you, I want twenty percent of the sale price for my fee." Eldritch opened.

"She still has all her guns and sails; I think ten percent will be enough." Fletcher replied.

Eldridge looked at him steadily and held out his hand.

"Fifteen percent and we have an accord."

Fletcher looked at Marty who nodded, "Agreed," and shook the man's hand.

"Now get her over here to my yard and I can get her cleaned up ready for sale." Eldridge said as he poured them all a glass of port.

The three of them left the boatyard slightly worse for wear as Eldridge turned out to be quite generous with his port and wanted to catch up with any news they had of England. They decided that a good dinner was what was needed so they selected a nice-looking restaurant and sat at a table. Blaez plonked himself down underneath and waited for the titbits to arrive.

The proprietor came over and explained what was on offer.

"Tonight, gentlemen you are extremely lucky. We have fresh caught Sea Bream, Flounder and Dabs, lobster and brown crab. On the meats we have a fresh roasted side of beef, young lamb, and some Spanish pork. Can I suggest you have onion soup to set your stomachs up right, followed by flounder cooked in butter with shallots, a selection of meats with potatoes and fresh greens and finish with our special Muscadet Posset and cheeses?"

They could only agree as they were drooling with hunger. They were served with a delicate Spanish white wine to go with the soup. The fish was everything that was promised, delicate, swimming in a white wine and butter sauce with very finely chopped shallots and brown crab meat sautéed into it and served with a salad. The meat course was substantial, with rare beef, pink cooked lamb and, to their surprise, slightly pink pork. They were assured it had been killed just that morning and was perfectly safe. Safe or not it was delicious! Like all sailors they found the vegetables most interesting and the cabbage had been lightly sautéed with nutmeg (one of the most expensive spices you could buy) grated over it. There were carrots and boiled onions as well.

The Muscadet Posset was sweet, alcoholic and refreshing. The selection of cheeses was unusual as they were all local and nothing like the cheeses they got in England.

By the time they finally finished it was quite late and they were so full they could hardly walk. They found a boatman who could ferry them to The Tempest and made it onboard by ten o'clock.

Chapter 23: A Craftsman At Work

The next morning Fletcher went ashore with Shelby to stock up on vegetables, fruit, medicines and livestock for the trip across the Atlantic. Shelby was fascinated by Fletcher's skill at getting the best possible price and Fletcher was educated by Shelby on what to buy to keep the men healthy. Shelby surprised Fletcher by asking him to help buy a pair of pistols and short sword similar to Marty's. When he asked him why, he answered that he didn't feel that he could ask Marty for any of the bodies the others had killed, for him to perform autopsies on but if he killed them himself it would probably be alright.

Fletcher choked a bit on that idea at first, but Shelby explained that one had to know one's way around a body if one wanted to heal it or mend any damage that had been done to it. He also explained there were gaps in his knowledge that could only be filled by dissection.

They visited the hospital and once he had introduced himself Shelby was invited to examine a man with acute stomach pains which he identified as an inflammation of the appendix. He told that he had witnessed an operation by Professor Claudius Amyand in London hospital to remove one. The doctor asked him if he could show them the procedure and Shelby agreed.

Fletcher discovered in himself a morbid fascination to see what they did and made his way to theatre where the operation would take place. He was accompanied by a couple of student doctors and sat in the tiered seats around the central operating area.

The doctors entered dressed in their normal day clothes and the poor patient was brought in on a stretcher which was just placed on the table. Shelby was the only one to wash his hands in brandy that he got from a flask in his pocket. The man on the table was in obvious agony and was only partially sedated by a large dose of Laudanum. Several burly attendants held him down and secured him with straps.

Shelby stepped forward and said. "May I?" The local doctor stepped aside and watched as Shelby carefully made an incision about four inches long in the man's abdomen, followed by two more incisions through the muscles to expose the intestine. He then inserted a tool that held the wound wide open and swabbed the blood away with a clean cloth. He delicately reached inside the wound with his fingers and pulled up a section of the intestine. Fletcher couldn't see what he did next, but he was sure he used a piece of catgut to tie something off and then cut it off above the tie. He deposited the severed piece in a dish and then proceeded to stitch up each layer of the abdomen in turn finishing with the skin. He washed the wound finally with brandy and dusted it with sulphur before they bandaged it.

The man was immediately quieter after the procedure and all the doctors shook hands with and congratulated Shelby on his work.

"Will he live?" asked Fletcher as they walked back to the port.

"He has a reasonable chance." Shelby answered. "The appendix had not perforated so there is little chance of internal infection. He could be up and about in a couple of weeks."

Back on The Tempest the two men were kept busy inventorying the stores and new medicines that were delivered. The story of the operation flew around the ship and Shelby found he was an object of ship wide pride. When he asked Marty about that he was told, "Sailors are a funny lot and very loyal to their ship. You have added kudos to their world as they now have something to brag about which can elevate this ship above others. No doubt the tale will be embellished and enlarged in the telling until you could be attributed divine powers."

Shelby looked horrified.

"Don't worry Shelby, you will look good in a halo." Marty joked.

All stores loaded and fresh water in the casks they set sail for Madeira. The wind was strong and from the Southwest which meant they were beating against it for several days before it swung more to the West. The sea was rough with big rollers pushing in from the West. This caused the ship to corkscrew as she made her way Southwest and sent both Fletcher and Shelby to their cabins with acute seasickness.

That ended abruptly, when a topman slipped when reefing a sail, was stopped from falling to the deck by the reefing line which had tangled around his wrist. The dislocated shoulder he got as a result meant that four of his fellow topmen had to manhandle him down to the deck. Once they got him below Shelby was rousted out of his cabin and found the topman's watch arrayed around the victim looking at him with almost religious expectation.

He didn't even realise his sickness had stopped, they gave him such a fright, but his professional self, kicked in and he went to work.

"What is your name?" he asked the man.

"Stanford Sir," he answered through clenched teeth.

"Well Mr Stanford," he continued as he examined the shoulder which stuck out at a very odd angle, "have you ever done this before?"

"No Sir."

"Well we are going to have to put that back where it belongs."

Shelby went to a chest, dug around a little and took out a wooden ball about four inches in diameter. He looked at the assembled men and pointing at the two biggest, asked them to hold the man around the chest and waist while he was sat on the floor. He then took the ball and placed it under the displaced arm in the armpit.

Taking a leather strap out of the chest he put it between Stanford's teeth and told him to bite down. The ship gave another lurch causing them all to pause and when it settled Shelby told another hand to hold the ball in place while he took Stanford's arm and manipulated it. He placed his foot on his ribcage and heaved back on the arm to pull it out, then using the ball as a pivot, got it lined up with the joint and allowed the shoulder to gently slide back into place with a slight pop.

Stafford never made a sound, but the tears were streaming down his face and he was soaked in sweat by the time it was over. Shelby then strapped his arm in place across his chest in a sling. It was all done between lurches.

"No climbing or hauling until that settles back into place," he cautioned and gave Stafford a large glass of brandy. "You will have one hell of a bruise later," he handed over a small jar of green paste, "you can rub some of this arnica ointment into it and that will help it heal."

The men left, each one touching his forelock and saying. "Thank you, Sir."

Chapter 24: The Last Leg

They reached Madeira and entered the port of Funchal, overlooked by an impressive fort. They again topped off their water and loaded up with fresh fruit and vegetables. Marty put the word out they were taking on men and they got another couple of experienced hands that had been left on the island for one reason or another.

The next leg was down to The Canaries which would be the last stop before the turned west and made for Tobago. At every stop Marty sent letters to Caroline, Miss Katy and his family. He didn't expect to get any from home until he had been in the Caribbean for a while. They would call in at English harbour every now and then to see if any had arrived.

They arrived in Tenerife and called into Santa Cruz. Marty just wanted to make sure they had as much fresh food and water as possible for the crossing so it was as short a stop as he could make it before they set off.

In consultation with the master he had decided to sail to Cape Verde and pick up the North Equatorial Current rather than try and go straight across. The advantage being if the wind died, the current would carry them on.

They stayed within sight of the African coast following the Canary current and swung more west towards the islands. Marty didn't want to stop there if they didn't have to, he was violently opposed to slavery and Cape Verdi was a centre for the trade.

They had just made the turn to the West when a huge storm hit them. The wind was shrieking down from the Northeast and they could do nothing but run before it. The waves were enormous, and The Tempest was picked up by the stern as they rolled beneath her until they got to the crest then they felt as if they were sliding backwards down the back of the wave until they reached the trough.

The helmsmen were worked hard keeping the ship with the wind on its stern and not letting her get side on to the seas. At the top of the waves they were exposed to the full fury of the wind but in the troughs, they were shaded from the direct force and almost stopped.

The hull flexed and leaked so they were having to pump for four hours, twice a day to keep her dry. It was exhausting work and it seemed it would never end.

Shelby had a constant stream of minor injuries to deal with including the occasional broken limb, concussion or rupture. He overcame his seasickness and dealt with every case increasing his reputation, becoming something of a talisman. As long as Shelby was with them, they were invincible.

The storm raged for a week and by the time it ended they were far Southwest of their planned course somewhere off the coast of Brazil. Marty, James and the Master managed to get a noon sighting and they all recalculated it twice before they believed it. They were South of the equator!

They set a course due West and sailed until they picked up the coast then turned North. They came upon a town and entered the bay to ask its name. As soon as they dropped anchor a host of bum boats came out that were offering everything, from fruit to women, to the crew. Paul La Pierre walked around the sides and had his men positioned to make sure no alcohol or women came aboard.

Fletcher bought fruit and asked where they were. He reported back to Marty and the master that the town was called Recife. They both peered at the map in vain until Marty got a magnifying glass from his cabin and they both peered again.

The Master jabbed a finger on the map.

"There! That's Recife." he said.

He got out the dividers and measured of the distance. They had another two thousand seven hundred miles to go and if they could maintain ten knots that would take another twelve days. Realistically he knew it would be at least two weeks before they hit English Harbour.

"Tom! Get a watering party organised. Top up the butts we won't be stopping again," he said. There was a squeal and a splash, then a stream of Portuguese invective. Marty walked down the deck and looked over the side to where the noise was coming from. There was a rather pretty woman swimming towards a boat that was edging towards her. Marty looked around and saw John Smith leaning against the foremast cleaning his fingernails with his knife. He didn't need to ask.

The watering party made several trips as they emptied the stale water from the casks and scoured them with sand before sending them to be filled. Once it was completed Marty set sail and they headed North. The easy thing to do would have been to follow the coast but Marty decided to 'cut the corner' and sail direct to Tobago then follow the islands up to Antigua.

The weather was kind with clear days and steady winds. The heat was something else and Shelby had multiple cases of sunburn to deal with. He had been told in Recife about a plant called Aloe which had a sap that soothed burns and cooled the skin. He had procured as much as he could much to the amusement of the crew, but they soon changed their tune when he started applying the cooling sap to their blistered skin.

They first landfall was eleven days later, and they identified it as Tobago. They turned to a couple of points West of North and followed the islands staying on the Atlantic side.

Another five days saw them entering English Harbour and dropping anchor. They had arrived.

Epilogue

Back in England two old men sat in front of a fire and discussed the state of the war.

"We have the French bottled up in Brest and Toulon but it will only take a storm from the wrong direction and they will get out," said Admiral Lord Hood.

"Yes, and we are still getting reports that Napoleon is building his troops up at the channel ports and they are building barges by the dozen" replied William Wickham. "They are still making those damn balloons as well."

"Martin's little bout of pyromania didn't stop that then?" Hood asked.

"No, they just moved the places they make and inflate them away from the troop encampments." Wickham sighed.

"Well as long as we command the seas between here and France they won't invade, it would be suicide." Hood observed and sipped his Brandy. "How is young Wellesley doing?"

"He has trumped that fellow Holkar and now the East India Company controls most of Southern India. He wrote that Martin did an excellent job and they have had very little trouble with pirates lately. Well none the Marine can't handle anyway." Wickham replied.

"Capital. Capital. By the way did you hear some Cornish fellow made a steam engine that could travel on the road?" Hood asked. "Damn fellow will be putting one in a ship next."

"Yes, read it in the Times. Stupid thing blew up, wouldn't do in a ship, and you wouldn't get me on one if they did." Wickham replied. "Have you heard from Martin?"

"Yes, he arrived in Madeira five weeks ago and was on his way to Antigua."

Hood replied. "A toast. To the end of piracy in the West Indies! May Martin create confusion, mayhem and fire!"
The two drained their glasses and smiled at the thoughts the toast inspired.

"Another Brandy?" Wickham asked.

Author's Note

It was fun writing this episode of Marty's adventures as I had to research what was happening in India at the time and try and build a story around it. Why wasn't it set in Europe? Well the problem with peace, or even impending peace is that not a lot happens in a military or even intelligence sense so I had to send Marty somewhere he would have something interesting to do. It gave me an excuse to put in some Indian food which I love. I also wanted to expand Caroline's role as well as the number of children. You can't go at it like those two do without it having consequences!

Arthur Wellesley is an interesting character. He has a reputation for being an unmitigated snob and having no time for the filthy lower classes. But that is in direct contradiction to his abilities as a military leader. He prided himself on not wasting his men's lives and for making sure he had the logistics of every campaign worked out before he started. You don't win wars with sick or starving men and no ammunition. He could also spot talent when he saw it. In the end I am happy with my version of him.

Returning to England at the resumption of the war he learned that command is not always easy, and that failure has its consequences. The Navy was intolerant of failure or shyness in combat. It had built its reputation on ruthless aggressiveness.

Finally, I would just like to say thank you to all of those who pre-ordered this book you give me the energy to keep writing.

Please check out the website, you can chat to me there or on The Dorset Boy Facebook page. I will always answer as soon as I can.

And now! A short preview of book 5

Book 5 - The Tempest

Chapter 1: Unhappy landings

The Tempest dropped anchor in English Harbour and Marty looked around in surprise it was just a Navy base and it stank! The lagoon was as filthy as a cesspit with the accumulated sewage from a couple of thousand people and the debris from careened warship hulls. There was no current and very little tide, so the filth just stayed there. *Shelby is the only one who will enjoy stopping here.* He thought as he saw the Physician at the rail taking notes.

Marty and his new ship, The Tempest, had been tasked to investigate, infiltrate and disrupt the pirate activity that had recently surged in the Caribbean. The Tempest was a former Navy Jackass Frigate, which was, to all intents and purposes, a Sloop of War with a raised quarterdeck. They had fitted her with bigger guns and carronades including two twenty-four-pound chasers, a natty set of red sails and a crew of one hundred and fifty men for the trip over to the Caribbean. His main concern now was to boost that to around two hundred.

He had left his wife, Lady Caroline Candor, behind in England with their two children. He had brought his dog Blaez with him who was sat beside him on the quarterdeck sniffing the air not quite sure if he liked the smell or not.

Where were all the people and a town? *I should have done more research, he* thought with a mental grimace *I'm not going to find more crew here.*

He consulted with Tom and James and decided to talk to the Yard Commissioner. He was one of their contacts for passing reports through and was appointed by the Navy Board. Admiral Hood had told them that the Honourable Francis Chapman was the current incumbent and he had written to him asking for his assistance.

Marty had the boys take him over in the gig, Tom joked that he could have walked the water was so thick with shit and made his way up the hill to the Clarence House the home of the Commissioner. He knocked on the door and a black house slave answered it. Marty asked to see the commissioner and was shown into what was obviously a waiting room. *At least its cooler in here* he thought as he sat and waited.

After an hour, during which he wasn't offered refreshments, he was ushered into an office. It was functional but he noticed that the cut glass decanter set and glasses on the sideboard was very good quality but a little too flashy for good taste. There was a picture of King George was pretty standard but the gilt frame too loud.

He was brought to attention by a cough and turned to see a man in an outdated powdered wig stood behind the desk, which was also a little ostentatious in its carving.

"Mr Chapman, I am pleased to meet you," he said as he stepped forward holding out his hand. "Martin Stanwell at your service."

The man didn't take the offered hand but replied as he sat down.

"Mr Chapman succumbed to fever some two months ago I am Seymour Owen. I am acting commissioner until the Navy Board either makes me permanent or designates another to the post," he said with a hint of bitterness in his voice.

Marty took an instant dislike to the man, which was unusual as he normally waited to form an opinion before judging. But his offhand manner and rudeness rankled with Marty's sense of correctness.

"Mr Chapman had been in contact with Admiral Lord Hood I believe concerning my, aah, business here. Did he mention anything about it to you?" Marty enquired, caution making him reticent.

Owen made a show of shuffling some papers.

"Why would Lord Hood be sending messages here about you?" he asked.

Alarm bells were going off in Marty's head, so he procrastinated.

"I am sponsored by the old fellow. He got me my letter of marque and helped fund my expedition."

"Letter of marque you say? Then you are a privateer?" Owen replied suddenly looking sly.

"Why yes," Marty replied. "Mr Chapman was to help me send my reports back to Admiral Hood so he could keep abreast of our progress."

"Please sit Mr Stanwell we have some business to discuss."

Printed in Great Britain
by Amazon

40297554R00128